UNNATURAL QUOTATIONS

Tennessee Williams • Michelangelo • Tallulah Bankhead • Joan Baez • Billie
Jean King • Rod McKuen • Michael Denneny • Christopher Isherwood • Boy
George • James Brolin • James Purdy • *The Tales of the Arabian Nights* • Al Gold-
stein • Corky Jones • Mart Crowley • Norman Mailer • Gore Vidal • Tennessee
Williams • Germaine Greer • Jean-Paul Sartre • Thomas Meyer • Frederick the
Great • Joe Orton • Hart Crane • Arthur Bell • Joseph Bottoms • Margaret
Mead • Gore Vidal • Richard Burton • Milton Berle • Jimmy Carter • Lillian
Carter • Renaud Camus • Quentin Crisp • Norman Mailer • Dale Evans •
Mike Royko • Martin Duberman • Harvey Milk • Winnie Mathews • Jack
Wyrtzen • C.S. Lewis • Erv Raible • W. Somerset Maugham • Truman Capote
• Kate Mill[   ] • Malcolm
Boyd • Johi[   ]eif • Frank
Zappa • Tr[   ] • Charles
Higham • /[   ]mingway •
Robert Patr[   ]oe Namath
• Donald Su[   ] Brando •
Richard Bu[   ]ruscott IV
• Gary Cart[   ]Ed Koch •

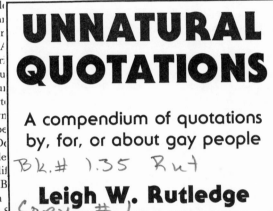

Jerry Brown[   ]Bankhead
• Albert Spe[A compendium of quotations]ine • John
Lennon • D[by, for, or about gay people]b Guccione
• Simone de[   ]in • Andre
Breton • Cli[Bk.# 1.35 Rut   ]ohn Henry
Mackay • B[   ]dal • John
Erlichmann [**Leigh W. Rutledge**   ]en • Clint
Eastwood • [Copy #1   ]ael Jackson
• Boy George • Christine Jorgensen • Mel Gibson • W.H. Auden • Madonna •
Mae West • Dave Diamond • Solon • Carl Van Vechten • Edmund White •
William S. Burroughs • Hustlers' Bar Graffiti • Richard Barnfield • Quentin
Crisp • Sting • Robert Bauman • Reynolds Price • W. Somerset Maugham •
Ken Russell • Andre Gide • Cyndi Lauper • Armistead Maupin • Richard
Locke • Luchino Visconti • Harvey Fierstein • John Updike • Anita Loos •
Harvard Coed • Clay Smothers • Myron Leavitt • Abigail Van Buren • Morris
Knight • Colt Thomas • Greg Jackson • John Hammond • Jerry Falwell • Oscar
Wilde • Bette Midler • Terry Sweeney • Richard Friedel • Dr. La Forest Potter
• Jack Hyles • Eddie Murphy • Sally Gearhart • Louisa Whitman • Jerry
O'Dowd • *Parting Glances* • Laura Z. Hobson • George Will • Dr. Benjamin
Spock • Dr. Wardell Pomeroy • Larry King • Tom Reeves • Cecil Beaton •
Harvey Fierstein • Quentin Crisp • Aaron Fricke • Paul Guilbert • Elton John •
Armistead Maupin • Al Parker • Laura Z. Hobson • Andrew Holleran • John
Schlesinger • Martha Shelley • Dr. Richard Pillard • Boy George • F. Scott Fitz-
gerald • Helen Gurley Brown • Jon-Erik Hexum • Robert Peters • Christopher
Isherwood • Edmund White • Jean Genet • Voltaire • Roy Garrett • Harold
Norse • Richard Locke • James Broughton • Plato • Jean Genet • Kristen Bjorn
• Andy Warhol • Roger Peyrefitte • Peter Berlin • Juvenal • St. Augustine •
Gore Vidal • Ned Rorem • Alan Watts • Valerie Perrine • Leontyne Price
• James Broughton • Vincent Van Gogh • Arstippus • Rudolph Valentino
• Andre Gide • Joe Orton • Cecil Beaton • Martin Greif • Noel Coward •
Addaeus of [   ] Stein • Dr.
David Reub **Boston • Alyson Publications** Leonardo da
Vinci • Eileen Farrell • Richard Locke • Arnie Kantrowitz • Peter Fisher • Tom
of Finland • Dr. Alfred Kinsey • Paul Goodman • Remy de Gourmont • Dolly

Portraits of Mark Twain, Eleanor Roosevelt, Herman Melville
and Oliver Wendell Holmes are reproduced from
The Dictionary of American Portraits,
published by Dover Publications, Inc., in 1967.

Portraits of Peter Ilyich Tchaikovsky and Benjamin Britten are
reproduced from *Great Composers in Historic Photographs,*
published by Dover Publications, Inc., in 1981.

Portraits of Tallulah Bankhead, Mae West and Johnny
Weissmuller are reproduced from *Hollywood Glamor Portraits,*
published by Dover Publications, Inc., in 1976.

The portrait of Orson Welles is reproduced from
Movie Star Portraits of the Forties,
published by Dover Publications, Inc., in 1977.

The portrait of John Wayne is reproduced from
Movie Star Portraits of the Fifties
published by Dover Publications, Inc., in 1980.

Published as a trade paperback original by
Alyson Publications
40 Plympton Street
Boston, Massachusetts 02118

Distributed in the U.K. by GMP Publishers,
PO Box 247, London, N15 6RW, England.

First U.S. edition: November, 1988

ISBN 1-55583-140-0

Unnatural Quotations
editor: Sasha Alyson
production: Wayne Curtis
design: Sasha Alyson and Wayne Curtis
proofreading: Tina Portillo
printing: McNaughton & Gunn Lithographers

CONTENTS

Valentino . . . Andre Gide . . . Joe Orton . . . Cecil Beaton . . .
Martin Greif . . . Noel Coward . . . Addaeus of Macedonia . . .
John Addington Symonds . . . Gertrude Stein . . . Dr. David
Reuben . . . Gore Vidal . . . *The Thing With Two Heads* . . .
Duncan Regehr . . . Leonardo da Vinci . . . Eileen Farrell . . .
Richard Locke . . . Tennessee Williams . . . Arnie Kantrowitz
. . . Peter Fisher . . . Tom of Finland . . . Frederick the Great . . .
Dr. Alfred Kinsey . . . Paul Goodman . . . Remy de Gourmont

VI. OSCAR WILDE: page 72

Oscar Wilde . . . Willie Wilde . . . Lord Alfred Douglas . . .
Oscar Wilde . . . Male Prostitute . . . Lord Alfred Douglas . . .
Oscar Wilde . . . Sir Alfred Wills . . . Oscar Wilde . . . Female
Prostitute . . . *Daily Telegraph* . . . W.H. Auden . . . Oscar Wilde
. . . W.T. Stead . . . Colonel George Keppel . . . Constance
Wilde . . . Oscar Wilde . . . Noel Coward . . . Joe Orton . . .
Laurence Housman . . . Oscar Wilde . . . Wilde's Epitaph . . .
Goldie Hawn . . . Algernon Swinburne

VII. ENTERTAINERS AND THE ENTERTAINED: page 79

Dolly Parton . . . Grace Jones . . . Maureen McGovern . . .
Bette Davis . . . Patti La Belle . . . Sophia Loren . . . Blake
Edwards . . . Paul Newman . . . Robert Towne . . . Kathleen
Nolan . . . Mamie Van Doren . . . John Wayne . . . Mike Con-
nors . . . Kirk Douglas . . . Dirk Bogarde . . . Richard Burton . . .
Rex Harrison . . . Michael Kearns . . . Gay Television Producer
. . . Johnny Mathis . . . Rock Hudson . . . Christopher Isherwood
. . . Vito Russo . . . Liz Smith . . . Ed Asner . . . Elton John . . .
Perry King . . . Harry Hamlin . . . Gene Barry . . . Michael
Caine . . . Charlie Sheen . . . David Hemmings . . . Michel Ser-
rault . . . John Dukakis . . . Cliff Gorman . . . Richard Gere . . .
Peter Finch . . . Armistead Maupin . . . Barry Sandler . . . James
Ivory . . . Raquel Welch . . . Mariel Hemingway . . . Letter to *In
Touch* . . . Bing Crosby . . . Jack LaLanne . . . Maureen
O'Sullivan . . . Fran Lebowitz . . . Mel Brooks

VIII. WORD OF MOUTH: page 94

George Bernard Shaw . . . Anita Bryant . . . Dr. Harry
Benjamin . . . E.M. Forster . . . Colette . . . Samuel Steward . . .
Ronald Reagan . . . Divine . . . Lanie Kazan . . . Dianne Fein-
stein . . . Robert L. Livingston . . . Armistead Maupin . . .
Liberace . . . Boy George . . . Joan Rivers . . . John Rechy . . .
John Waters . . . Dolly Parton . . . Quentin Crisp . . . Gore Vidal

Russo ... Robert M. Moore ... Frank DiPrima ... Michael
Diamond ... *Newsweek* ... Sue Caves ... Peter Jennings ...
Kurt Marshall

paedia Britannica ... Willa Cather ... H.L. Mencken ...
Oliver Wendell Holmes ... Oscar Wilde ... Mart Crowley ...
Pauline Kael ... Arthur Bell ... *The Advocate* ... *Glen or Glenda?*
... Magnus Hirschfeld ... Christopher Marlowe ... William
Shakespeare ... Plato ... Don Jackson ... Anti-Vietnam War
Poster ... Martin Luther ... Justinian ... Bruce Voeller ...
Gregg Howe ... Dan White ... Robin Tyler ... Greil Marcus
... Spectator at Dan White Trial ... P. Thomas Cary ... Frank
Rizzo ... Tom Waddell

To SAM, of course

FOREWORD AND ACKNOWLEDGEMENTS

"By necessity, by proclivity, and by delight, we all quote," Emerson once wrote, and it is probably truer today than it was a hundred and twelve years ago. Quotes — in magazines, newspapers, and books — have become big business: consumers are insatiable to read what celebrities, politicians, and self-described "experts" have to say about world peace, AIDS, the environment, the Academy Awards, and each other. There is barely a general interest magazine in the country that has not, in the last three or four years, added a small monthly or weekly column of notable quotes to its layout.

This minor obsession with quotes seems, for whatever reason, particularly pronounced in the gay community. When I first came out and started going to gay bars, I remember being bombarded with quotes: lines from Bette Davis movies, lines from plays, quotable nuggets from recent interviews and gossip columns, as well as the inevitable assortment of *bon mots* (often misquoted) from the patron saint of the one-liner, Oscar Wilde. I even once had a brief (very brief) romantic fling with a man who spoke in almost nothing but quotes. No matter what you said to him — about the weather, about movies, about a desirable man standing ten feet away — he began virtually every sentence with, "Well, as Joyce Carol Oates once said..." or "As Flaubert once remarked to a beggar..."

Why then should I participate in the fray? I suppose it goes back to Emerson: by necessity, by proclivity, and by delight. By necessity and proclivity, because most of us are eager to know

11

how our favorite celebrity stands on the issue of gay rights, and what, if anything, Imelda Marcos or Gertrude Stein or George Bernard Shaw had to say about homosexuality. By delight, because there are few things in the world more satisfying to the brain than the penetrating one-liner, the insightful, gem-like quote, and few things more delicious than the spectacle of the pompous movie star or ambitious senator revealing his or her true self to the world in a remark whose mangled reasoning alternately makes us howl with laughter and cringe with disbelief. Whatever gains gay people have made in the last twenty years, we should remember there are an appalling number of very stupid and very frightening people who know virtually nothing about homosexuality, or the whys and wherefores of being gay, but who, through their daily pronouncements, help to influence public opinion. We should also remember that there are many well-known people who, with a passing remark in an interview or a pointed rejoinder in public, have helped to eradicate stereotypes about gay people.

I considered many different ways to organize this book: chronologically, or by subject, or alphabetically by author. But more than a reference volume, I wanted this book to be a symposium of sorts — a dialogue — and I wanted it to be an entertainment: thought-provoking, and at times titillating or astonishing or maddening, but an entertainment nonetheless. For that reason, it is not exhaustive (how much value would there have been in quoting *every* celebrity and politician who has said "Gay is good" or "Gay is bad," as the case may be?), and it certainly reflects my own interests and prejudices. Also, this book, like *The Gay Book of Lists*, is aimed primarily at a gay male audience; a lesbian book of quotations must come from someone else.

Throughout the book, I have used only quotes from sources generally considered reliable. Aside from many biographies and historical sources, the publications most heavily relied on here have been: *The New York Times*, *Playboy*, *The Advocate*, *Newsweek*, *The Wall Street Journal*, *Rolling Stone*, *People*, *Christopher Street*, *Esquire*, and *Time*, athough dozens of publications, ranging from *The New Yorker* to *Gay Sunshine*, have been used. Works by interviewers with a reputation for unreliability (and, sadly, there are many) or publications with a general reputation for unreliability have been avoided. Because this is primarily an entertainment and not a reference book as such, a bibliography, running to over six hundred items, seemed unwieldy and impractical. Anyone interested in the source of a specific quote is free to write me at the address below.

For their help in providing me with information or assistance, I would like to take a moment to thank: M. Beardsley, Richard Donley, Myron O. Mercure, Cameron and Stacee Milani, John Phelps, Edward Rutledge, Chris Schick, Charlotte Simmons, Peter Urbanek, Neil Woodward of Category Six in Denver, and my publisher, Sasha Alyson. There are two people in particular to whom I owe an enormous debt for their help with this book. The first is Lola Milani, who helped many afternoons with research for the book, and then, when it came time, as we had earlier agreed, to pay her for her work, announced she would simply not accept payment in any form. To find such a friend is rare; to find such a friend in a next-door neighbor amounts to a minor miracle. The second is Sam Staggs, whose advice and encouragement every step of the way, and whose biweekly envelopes stuffed with clippings and research leads, were utterly invaluable.

As with *The Gay Book of Lists*, I would enjoy hearing from anyone who has comments, additions, questions, or even complaints about *Unnatural Quotations*. Those so inclined should write to:

Leigh W. Rutledge
P.O. Box 5523
Pueblo, Colorado 81002

OVERTURE

I imagine that sex between a man and a woman is probably a very beautiful thing. But you have to understand it's somethin' that's beyond me. When I was still a very young boy, I was taken to a whore house for my initiation into manhood, and this woman made me look right between her legs. I don't know, all I could see was somethin' that looked like a dyin' orchid. Consequently, I have never been comfortable either with orchids or women.

TENNESSEE WILLIAMS (1912-1983), to
actress Elizabeth Ashley

You must know that I am, of all men who were ever born, the most inclined to love persons. Whenever I behold someone who possesses any talent or displays any dexterity of mind, who can do or say something more appropriately than the rest of the world, I am compelled to fall in love with him; and then I give myself up to him so entirely that I am no longer my own property, but wholly his.

MICHELANGELO (1475-1564)

I don't know what I am, darling. I've tried several varieties of sex. The conventional position makes me claustrophobic. And the others give me either stiff neck or lockjaw.

Actress TALLULAH BANKHEAD
(1903-1968)

15

...if you thought I was left-wing, I'm not. If you thought I was right-wing, I'm not. If you thought I was queer, I'm not. If you thought I was stable, I'm not.

> *JOAN BAEZ, in a 1987 interview. Baez had a lesbian affair when she was twenty-two. As a result of her candor about it, she was, in her words, "absolutely inundated at my concerts with homosexual women; and really, I am not interested."*

I hate being called a homosexual because I don't feel that way. It really upsets me ... Being gay can happen in any walk of life, in any world. If you have one gay experience, does that mean you're gay? If you have one heterosexual experience, does that mean you're straight? Life doesn't work quite so cut and dried.

> *Tennis pro BILLIE JEAN KING, who acknowledged in 1981 that she had had a lesbian affair with her former hairdresser and secretary, Marilyn Barnett*

I've had sex with men. Does that make me gay?

> *ROD McKUEN*

Homosexuality and gay are not the same thing; gay is when you decide to make an issue of it.

> *Writer and editor MICHAEL DENNENY*

It seems to me that the real clue to your sex-orientation lies in your romantic feelings rather than in your sexual feelings. If you are really gay, you are able to fall in love with a man, not just enjoy having sex with him.

> *CHRISTOPHER ISHERWOOD*
> *(1904-1986)*

There's this illusion that homosexuals have sex and heterosexuals fall in love. That's completely untrue. Everybody wants to be loved.

> *BOY GEORGE*

I feel God made two sexes, and they fit together perfectly. A penis and a penis doesn't fit. A vagina and a vagina doesn't fit. And that's because a penis is made for only one thing — a snatch. The two parts are literally made for each other, and anyone who tries to deviate from that is defying nature.

Actor JAMES BROLIN

————

Of course, those who say heterosexuality is somehow better are all wrong; of course that isn't so. D.H. Lawrence started all that bosh — if you put it in a hole that somehow solves everything. It doesn't solve anything. There *are* no solutions: that's the human condition.

Writer JAMES PURDY

————

The penis smooth and round was made
With anus best to match it;
Had it been made for cunnus' sake
It had been formed like a hatchet.

*From THE TALES OF THE ARABIAN
NIGHTS, translated by Sir Richard F.
Burton, 1888*

————

The faggots who work in my office . . . say the sphincter muscle is a great source of pleasure. I would be ashamed to be fucked in the ass; or maybe I'm just afraid I'd like it.

AL GOLDSTEIN, editor and publisher of
Screw *magazine*

————

In theory, all men are makeable. I have yet to meet a straight man who didn't like a blow job. Without any exaggeration, it's like dangling a carrot in front of a donkey's nose. They're a little slower about buttfucking, but if you can put the man in the right frame of mind, you can get anything out of him.

*Writer CORKY JONES, in a 1980 article
"How to Pick Up Straight Men"*

With the right wine and the right music there're damn few that aren't curious.

Larry, in MART CROWLEY's play
The Boys in the Band, *1968*

There is probably no sensitive heterosexual alive who is not preoccupied with his latent homosexuality.

NORMAN MAILER

There is no such thing as a homosexual, no such thing as a heterosexual. Everyone has homosexual and heterosexual desires and impulses and responses ... But trust a nitwit society like this one to think that there are only two categories — fag and straight — and if you're the first, you want to be a woman, and if you're the second, you're a pretty damned wonderful guy ... Very few so-called fags are feminine in their ways and very few heteros can be regarded as wonderful.

GORE VIDAL

We are *not* trying to imitate women.

TENNESSEE WILLIAMS

To tell you the truth, I think every man should be fucked up the arse as a prelude to fucking women, so that he'll know what it's like to be the receiver.

Feminist GERMAINE GREER

The rump is the secret femininity of males, their passivity.

JEAN-PAUL SARTRE (1905-1980)

I like opening up. I like all the tensing and relaxing of muscle and meat that fucking demands. I want *it* — in this case, a cock — inside me, going deep. Getting fucked gives me that feeling of openness, receptivity, and that fantastic sense of pulling something inside myself.

Poet THOMAS MEYER

Actor Joseph Bottoms: What goes around, comes around.

I can assure you, from my own personal experience, that this Greek pleasure is not a pleasant one to cultivate.

FREDERICK THE GREAT (1712-1786),
in a letter to his nephew

———

You must do whatever you like as long as you enjoy it and don't hurt anybody else. That's all that matters . . . You shouldn't feel guilty. Get yourself fucked if you want to. Get yourself anything you like. Reject all the values of the society. And enjoy sex. When you're dead, you'll regret not having fun with your genital organs.

Playwright JOE ORTON (1933-1967),
to British actor Kenneth Williams, who
confided to Orton that he felt guilty about being
homosexual

———

Let my lusts be my ruin, then, since all else is a fake and a mockery.

Poet HART CRANE (1899-1932)

———

What we do in bed is still a great mystery to most heterosexuals . . . It's the sexual part of us that is the last boundary, and the biggest fear of straights.

Journalist ARTHUR BELL (1940-1984)

———

I don't hate gays, but I believe they're awfully unfulfilled human beings. I really think homosexuality is a dead-end street. It's self-adulation. It's masturbation . . . I feel sorry for them because they're unnatural.

Actor JOSEPH BOTTOMS, who portrayed a
gay football player in the NBC miniseries
Celebrity

———

I think extreme heterosexuality is a perversion.

Anthropologist MARGARET MEAD
(1901-1978), speaking before the Washington
Press Club in 1976

To hear two American men congratulating each other on being heterosexual is one of the most chilling experiences — and unique to the United States. You don't hear two Italians sitting around complimenting each other because they actually like to go to bed with women. The American is hysterical about his manhood.

GORE VIDAL

———

I have never known anyone who took great exception to homosexuals ... that there wasn't something drastically wrong with that very person himself.

RICHARD BURTON (1925-1984),
interviewed on the set of the 1969 film
Staircase, *in which he and Rex Harrison*
played a middle-aged gay couple

———

Listen, I don't know why the fuck they're beefing about the gays today. I never looked at it that way. It's your life, it's my life, it's the next one's — to do whatever we want with our fucking lives. We've got one life to live — let's live it the way we want to.

MILTON BERLE

———

The issue of homosexuality always makes me nervous ... I don't have any, you know, personal knowledge about homosexuality and I guess being a Baptist, that would contribute to a sense of being uneasy ... At home in Plains, we've had homosexuals in our community, our church. There's never been any sort of discrimination — some embarrassment but no animosity, no harassment.

Former President JIMMY CARTER

———

I don't know a gay from a hole in the ground — in my part of the country, we don't have 'em.

LILLIAN CARTER (1898-1983), mother of
Jimmy Carter

———

Homosexuality is always elsewhere because it is everywhere.

French writer RENAUD CAMUS

In an expanding universe, time is on the side of the outcast. Those who once inhabited the suburbs of human contempt find that without changing their address they eventually live in the metropolis.

> QUENTIN CRISP,
> The Naked Civil Servant, *1978*

What's happened to me is not remarkable. I think it is what's happened to half of America. There is a vast degree of tolerance. I used to look upon homosexuality as profound evil, and now I've gotten more modest. My feeling is, it is not for me to judge.

> *NORMAN MAILER*

I cannot sit in judgment of anyone. I have been forgiven a great deal myself. But there are some things that God just does not condone — and homosexuality is just one of them. It says so many times in the Bible.

> *Entertainer DALE EVANS,*
> *wife of cowboy star Roy Rogers*

If God dislikes gays so much, how come he picked Michelangelo, a known homosexual, to paint the Sistine Chapel ceiling while assigning Anita to go on TV and push orange juice?

> *Chicago columnist MIKE ROYKO*

It is fair to expect that if biblical fundamentalists are going to follow the dictates of *Leviticus* to the literal letter, they will show equal nicety in adhering to the rest of the "original" (pre-exegetical) biblical code of behavior. Which means they will no longer break the Sabbath by attending movies or by joining bowling parties. That they will no longer accumulate worldly goods beyond providing for basic needs (one doubts Anita Bryant's $300,000 mansion will qualify). That the men among them will grow luxuriant beards and the women silken hair on their legs. That they will no longer engage in any sexual act other than missionary intercourse — and then only when procreation is the goal.

Perhaps on one matter a little hypocrisy should be tolerated; since Kinsey has shown that more than half the male population had extramarital relations, we nonfundamentalists would not demand that adulterers be stoned to death in the streets. We, too, after all, are patriots: we do not wish to see the country decimated.

> *Historian MARTIN DUBERMAN*

———

The fact is that more people have been slaughtered in the name of religion than for any other single reason. That, that my friends, that is true perversion!

> *San Francisco City Supervisor*
> *HARVEY MILK (1930-1978), at a 1978*
> *Gay Freedom Day rally*

———

We would never advocate a stoning or a burning at the stake, as long as homosexuals keep their sexual preference in private.

> *WINNIE MATHEWS, conservative-religious*
> *delegate to the 1977 National Women's Confer-*
> *ence in Houston*

———

Homosexuality is a sin so rotten, so low, so dirty that even cats and dogs don't practice it.

> *JACK WYRTZEN, head of Word of Life*
> *International, an international Bible organiza-*
> *tion, during the 1977 battle over gay rights in*
> *Dade County, Florida*

———

There is much hypocrisy on this theme. People commonly talk as if every other evil were more tolerable than this. But why? Because those of us who do not share the vice feel for it a certain nausea, as we do, say, for necrophily? I think that of very little relevance to moral judgment.

> *British theological scholar and author*
> *C.S. LEWIS (1898-1963)*

———

It's strange that people judge you on only one part of your life.

After all, out of a 168-hour week, you might have sex for about two or three hours. And it's these three hours that form the basis of how a whole world looks at you and judges you.

West Village gay entrepreneur ERV RAIBLE

———

My own belief is that there is hardly anyone whose sexual life, if it were broadcast, would not fill the world at large with surprise and horror.

W. SOMERSET MAUGHAM
(1874-1965); Maugham once told his nephew,
"Why do you think that Noel [Coward] or I
have never stuck our personal predilections down
our public's throats? Because we know it would
outrage them. Believe me, I know what I'm
talking about."

———

I never had any problem with being a homosexual. I mean, look at me. I was always right out there.

TRUMAN CAPOTE (1924-1984)

———

Truman Capote: He told one interviewer that his attitude toward people put off by him was, "You think I'm different, well, I'll show you how different I really am."

We risk something taking up this life. In taking off on our own and in loving women, there's a bit of the lad in it; the adventurer.

Feminist and writer KATE MILLETT

I was so excited to be able to say that I was a lesbian that I would shake hands with strangers on the street and say, "Hi! I'm Sally Gearhart and I'm a lesbian." Once, appearing on a panel program, I began, "I'm Sally Lesbian and I'm a gearhart!" I realized then that I had put too much of my identity into being lesbian.

Feminist SALLY GEARHART

I never really liked phrases such as "Gay Pride" and "I'm *proud* to be a Homosexual" . . . One should not be forced to have pride in one's sexuality. Sexuality *is* for goshsakes. Imagine how foolish to be put in a position to have to say: "I am *proud* to drink water!"

Writer THANE HAMPTEN, in a 1970 article in Gay *magazine*

Anyone can be gay — it's no accomplishment — but only I can be me.

Composer NED ROREM

Homosexuality for thousands of years has been the unnameable leprosy. And in almost all cultures, it's been freely regarded as reason for torture, torment and terrible things. It's just the unnameable dreadful thing. For anyone to reach a level of self-esteem where one is actually proud of oneself, including that part, and able to see everything as God's creation, is what I would call tremendous.

Episcopal priest and gay activist MALCOLM BOYD

We maintain that we have the right to exist after the fashion which nature made us. And if we cannot alter your laws, we shall go on breaking them. You may condemn us to infamy, exile, prison — as you formerly burned witches. You may degrade our emotional instincts and drive us into vice and misery. But you will not eradicate inverted sexuality.

Victorian writer JOHN ADDINGTON
SYMONDS (1840-1893)

———

One woman asked me if toleration of the third sex would ever come, and I replied that Havelock Ellis thought there was a faint light in the darkness, but that it would probably not come in our lifetime. She wrote back saying, "I am just twenty-three — do you think it will be very long?" I could not help visualizing the many stony miles that her feet must tread.

RADCLYFFE HALL (1883-1943), com-
menting on one of the letters she received in
response to her novel The Well of Loneliness

———

That homosexuality has been a natural condition of kings, composers, engineers, poets, housewives, and bus drivers, and that it has contributed more than its share of beauty and laughter to an ugly and ungrateful world should be obvious to anyone who is willing to peer beneath the surface.

Writer MARTIN GREIF

———

My attitude toward anybody's sexual persuasion is this: without deviation from the norm, progress is not possible.

FRANK ZAPPA

REVELATIONS

I was a beautiful little boy ... and everyone had me — men, women, dogs, and fire hydrants. I did it with everybody. I didn't slow down until I was nineteen, and then I became very circumspect.

TRUMAN CAPOTE

I've been raped, yes, by a goddamn Mexican, and I screamed like a banshee and couldn't sit for a week. And once a handsome beachboy, very powerful, swam up on a raft, and he raped me in his beach shack. I had a very attractive ass and people kept wanting to *fuck* me that way...

TENNESSEE WILLIAMS

From my earliest childhood I was the Lillie Langtry of the older homosexual set. Everybody wanted me. I had a very bad way of turning these guys off. I thought it would embarrass them if I said I wasn't homosexual, that that would be a rebuke, so I always had a headache. You know, I was like an eternal virgin.

ORSON WELLES (1915-1985), who at an early age was often surrounded by gay men at his mother's artistic salons

---

The subject seemed to obsess him. He was not homosexual, but

Orson Welles: Being an eternal virgin meant a lot of headaches.

he had an intense fascination . . . I think this was in part because so many figures in his life were homosexual. Michael McClearmore, the late and great figure of the Gate Theatre of Dublin, and his lover, the late Hilton Edwards who ran the Gate, gave Welles his start. They were both homosexuals. One of Welles' lawyers was homosexual. There were others, a whole series of gay people who deeply influenced his life.

CHARLES HIGHAM,
one of Orson Welles' biographers

I became aware of the fact that there were a few homosexuals around bodybuilding. These were not the bodybuilders themselves, not the serious ones. Two or three rich guys in Munich hung out in the gyms and tried to pick up young bodybuilders by promising them the world. Some of them did accept. But I was never sorry I turned down the offers I had.

ARNOLD SCHWARZENEGGER

I never in my entire life had a gay man make a pass at me. I some-times wonder what the hell's wrong with *me*!

Science-fiction writer HARLAN ELLISON

———

I had certain prejudices against homosexuality since I knew its more primitive aspects. I knew it was why you carried a knife . . . You had to be prepared to kill a man, know how to do it and really know that you would do it in order not to be interfered with.

ERNEST HEMINGWAY (1899-1961)

———

I've met sixteen-year-old kids from Fresno who, not knowing I was gay, would smile at me and confide in me and reach inside their pants and pull out a switchblade knife and say, "I carry this around so I can cut up any queers I meet when I travel."

Playwright ROBERT PATRICK

———

Certainly, your average straight seems to exhibit a curious horror of homosexuality that makes no sense to me. Is it because of fear of discovering that one is homosexual? But why fear? Surely in love-making there should be no rules.

Science-fiction writer ALFRED BESTER

———

If we do violence to any part of ourselves, we do violence to other people. We all need to express the different forces in us: material-istic, mystic, sexual. If we keep down any one of these, it will come back as contempt, hatred, the desire to kill.

Poet HAROLD NORSE

———

There are certain types of women that I am attracted to . . . It's ridiculous for a woman to say that she's not attracted to other women. That's completely false . . . When does one decide whether it's sexual or mental? All of those relationships are some-times so closely related that one gets confused and doesn't really even know.

GRACE JONES

Joe Namath: He's thought about it, but, no, he isn't.

Am I gay? The hair on a woman's body excites me. I've never seen hair on a man's body that excites me in any way. I admit I've wondered. I've thought it over, thought about it over the years, vicariously, of course, putting myself in various positions, thinking them out. And it hasn't turned me on when I think about men in a sexual way.

> *JOE NAMATH*

The only kind of gay people I find attractive are those bordering on the transvestite.

> *DONALD SUTHERLAND*

...little by little, I found out that I was a very normal human being who might have had some homosexual fantasies and who had had what would be considered — and I hesitate to use the term — homosexual childhood adventures. They were perfectly normal explorations that we all do with other kids, but a lot of people won't even admit *that*.

> *BLAKE EDWARDS,*
> *director of* Victor/Victoria

Along the way I'd had homosexual encounters, but that kind of sex always felt unreal to me and unsatisfying.

> *ANTHONY PERKINS*

Homosexuality is so much in fashion it no longer makes news. Like a large number of men, I, too, have had homosexual experiences and I am not ashamed.

> *MARLON BRANDO, in a 1976 interview in*
> *Paris; responding to some critics' contentions*
> *that his film* The Missouri Breaks *was*
> *pervaded with homosexuality, Brando added, "I*
> *have never paid much attention to what people*
> *think about me. But if there is someone who is*
> *convinced that [co-star] Jack Nicholson and I*
> *are lovers, may they continue to do so. I find it*
> *amusing."*

Perhaps most actors are latent homosexuals and we cover it with drink. I was once a homosexual, but it didn't work.

RICHARD BURTON

———

Of course. Who hasn't? Good God! If anyone had ever told me that he hadn't, I'd have told him he was lying. But then, of course, people tend to "forget" their encounters.

Science-fiction writer ARTHUR C.
CLARKE, asked if he had ever had any
"bisexual experience"

———

The Christ-was-I-drunk-last-night syndrome. You know, when you made it with some guy in school and the next day when you had to face each other there was always a lot of shit-kicking crap about, "Man, was I drunk last night! Christ, I don't remember a thing!"

Michael, in MART CROWLEY's play The
Boys in the Band, *1968*

———

Homosexuality was as bizarre as seeing a gorilla walk down Fifth Avenue dressed up in a tuxedo ... People would have killed themselves in my early years before they would have had such a thing imputed to them ... Now, it is different — and, I think, much better. I don't think people should be persecuted for their sexual habits ... I believe in people doing what they need to do. Or want to do.

Writer JAMES DICKEY,
author of Deliverance

———

If it was found out that someone was gay, they just vanished. They were out of the academy within twenty-four hours. I know three guys that happened to. Hardly anyone knew about it. A couple of them were involved with officers, and they disappeared just as quickly. There was no scandal; they were just gone.

Writer LUCIAN TRUSCOTT IV, author of
Dress Gray, *on homosexuality at West Point*

The idea of grown men, athletes, touching each other may bring some chuckles here and there. But it isn't sexual. Bill Robinson, a Mets coach, and I have a ritual, which we call our "good-luck hug." I go into the clubhouse every night and look for Uncle Bill. "Hey," I'll say, "Where's my good luck hug?" He'll give it to me. It would take a very brave man to suggest that Uncle Bill and I have a gay streak.

New York Mets catcher GARY CARTER

People thought I must be gay. To keep from getting beat up, I studied fighting. I grew my hair long, in redneck Texas, mind you, then went around waiting for someone to throw a punch. I became a very angry young man.

Actor PATRICK SWAYZE, on his early days as a ballet dancer

You know I sort of knew when I started dancing that there was this sort of feeling that ballet dancers are gay. But I thought that was restricted to people in Podunk or the Deep South or something ... I pretty much figured that the cosmopolitan, civilized adult world didn't really get off on snickering about ballet dancers. Apparently, some of them still did.

RON REAGAN, former ballet dancer and son of President Ronald Reagan, on rumors about his sexuality; on another occasion, he told an interviewer, "It surprised me that there were people who still felt that dancing was non-masculine. There are gay truck drivers too, but nobody talks about that. It's just the fact that truck drivers don't wear tights."

He's all man — we made sure of that.

RONALD REAGAN, asked on the campaign trail in 1978 whether his son Ron was gay

---

I remain convinced, without knowing the actual figures, that a substantial number of people voted for me thinking I was homo-

Tallulah Bankhead: Pleading ignorance.

sexual. Equally, a substantial number voted for me thinking I'm *not* homosexual.

> *New York City Mayor ED KOCH*

———

Homosexual innuendo is a cheap shot that could be used against any single politician. It's like Red-baiting in the fifties. Now I'm accused of running around the state with too many women. You're damned if you do and damned if you don't.

> *Former California Governor JERRY BROWN*

———

People say that everybody is gay. California is the worst for that stuff . . . People want to hear ugliness.

> *Singer JERMAIN JACKSON,*
> *Michael Jackson's brother*

———

This is utterly ridiculous and preposterous. That charge surfaced in the homosexual press, which claimed everybody from Moses on up was a homosexual. If you had any idea of his New England background and his Catholicism, you would know it was a foolish charge.

> *MSGR. V. CLARK, private secretary to New*
> *York Archbishop Francis Cardinal Spellman*
> *(1889-1967), on stories that Spellman was a*
> *practicing homosexual*

———

I don't know, darling — he never sucked my cock.

> *TALLULAH BANKHEAD, when asked if*
> *an acquaintance of hers was gay*

———

I think that was just wartime propaganda, rather like the stories that he was of Jewish ancestry or chewed the carpets in epileptic fits or was a syphilitic. No, Hitler was sexually normal; his perversion was of the soul, not of the body.

> *Nazi architect and Hitler confidante ALBERT*
> *SPEER (1905-1981), on speculation that*
> *Hitler was homosexual*

I am not a lesbian and never have been, though I'm not putting those people down. Those pictures were choreographed to look that way. Sure, I know people think I'm a lesbian. Just the other day someone went by my house and said, "Oh, that's where the lesbian lives." But no matter how many boyfriends I bring out to testify that I'm not gay, people will only believe what they want to believe.

> *Former Miss America VANESSA*
> *WILLIAMS, forced to resign her crown in*
> *1984 after* Penthouse *magazine announced*
> *plans to publish nude pictures of her in erotic*
> *poses with another woman*

———

...you know, when Cristina Ford used to come here, everybody would say I was a lesbian ... One time, we were with Placido Domingo, the singer, and there were about twelve women at one round table, and all of them did not want to touch me with a ten-foot pole because I was such a queen of the lesbians.

> *IMELDA MARCOS, in a 1984 newspaper*
> *interview in Manila*

———

I could tell Christopher Reeve wasn't gay, because he didn't close his eyes when I kissed him.

> *MICHAEL CAINE, on his on-screen kiss*
> *with co-star Christopher Reeve in the 1982 film*
> Deathtrap

———

I went on holiday to Spain with Brian — which started all the rumors that he and I were having a love affair. Well, it was almost a love affair, but not quite. It was never consummated. But we did have a pretty intense relationship. And it was my first experience with someone I knew was a homosexual ... We used to sit in cafes and Brian would look at all the boys and I would ask, "Do you like that one? Do you like this one?" It was just the combination of our closeness and the trip that started the rumors.

> *JOHN LENNON (1940-1980), on rumors*
> *that he and manager Brian Epstein were lovers*

During the time I was doing the play, there were all kinds of stories and rumors that we were secretly lovers, but it was never true ... I think that Sal had an obsession with me, but he was always very respectful of my heterosexuality and my space, too, and was too much of a gentleman to let it get in the way.

> *Actor DON JOHNSON, on Sal Mineo,*
> *who directed Johnson in a stage production of*
> Fortune and Men's Eyes

I think you are wonderful and charming, and if I should ever change from liking girls better, you would be my first thought.

> *HUMPHREY BOGART (1899-1957),*
> *to Noel Coward*

I know lots of homosexuals who didn't discover their homosexuality until an advanced age ... There was one case I knew of, a marquis who only discovered he was gay at age forty-five. With fright! Then he realized he had lost forty years of his life. One should never lose hope. Homosexuality can strike any straight man at any age.

> *French novelist ROGER PEYREFITTE*

I think that a man who goes from genuinely straight to gay is a man who would feel that he has lost some terrible internal battle with himself, would feel that he had let himself down.

> Penthouse *publisher BOB GUCCIONE*

In itself, homosexuality is as limiting as heterosexuality: the ideal should be to be capable of loving a woman or a man; either, a human being, without feeling fear, restraint, or obligation.

> *French writer SIMONE DE BEAUVOIR*
> *(1908-1986)*

I'm a very sexual person and I prefer to describe myself as just being sexual. Not gay, not heterosexual, and not bisexual. Just sexual.

> *Porn star GLENN SWANN*

I'm a practicing heterosexual ... but bisexuality immediately doubles your chances for a date on Saturday night.

WOODY ALLEN

Actually, I think bisexuality is much more sane than being committed to being a heterosexual or a homosexual. Bisexuality is as natural as driving different-color cars. If I was renting from Avis or Hertz, it would be silly to express a preference only for black cars.

Editor and publisher AL GOLDSTEIN

I wish I could change my sex as I change my shirt.

French poet ANDRE BRETON (1896-1966)

So it is that nature makes of all of us indulgent monsters with Sir Instinct as chief pimp. And I have done monstrous things (if anything can be so adjectived) and will continue to do them as often as I have desire. I sense in myself as of old, every possible queerness: there is no sexual "depravity" in which I might not indulge at one time or another. I think the only sin is lack of selection, promiscuity...

*Playwright CLIFFORD ODETS
(1906-1963), who often struggled with what he
called "homosexual anxieties." Odets once wrote,
"I never see a man or a woman — when I am
happy — that I don't want to kiss them or at
least touch them with my hand."*

There are some people living their lives as homosexuals who would be happier if they realized they are heterosexuals. There are some people living their lives as heterosexuals who would be happier if they realized and accepted the fact that they are homosexuals. But everyone will be happier accepting himself as he is in the present and letting the future take care of itself.

Writer PETER FISHER,
The Gay Mystique, *1975*

Oh, you mean I'm homosexual! Of course I am, and heterosexual too. But what's that got to do with my headache?

> *Poet EDNA ST. VINCENT MILLAY*
> *(1892-1950), in response to a doctor who*
> *hinted that her severe recurring headaches might*
> *be due to repressed lesbian impulses*

After all, each person only understands his own love and every other is foreign and incomprehensible to him.

> *Early gay rights activist JOHN HENRY*
> *MACKAY (1864-1933)*

POTPOURRI

They are a very extensive minority who have suffered discrimination and who have the right to participation in the promise and the fruits of society as every other individual.

*Former Congresswoman BELLA ABZUG
(D-New York), at a 1975 press conference to
introduce a federal gay rights bill*

―――――

If gays are granted rights, next we'll have to give rights to prostitutes and to people who sleep with St. Bernards and to nailbiters.
ANITA BRYANT

―――――

Anita, you are to Christianity what paint-by-numbers is to art!
Entertainer ROBIN TYLER

―――――

As to Anita's fear that she'll be assassinated? The only people who might shoot Anita Bryant are music lovers.
GORE VIDAL

―――――

There are lots of gays who are pillars of the community, and they've become our friends. My wife Christy and I enjoy them as we do our straight friends. And I feel comfortable having my children around gays. After all, they've accepted me with all my problems.

Watergate conspirator
JOHN ERLICHMANN

———

Homosexuals make the best friends because they care about you as a woman and are not jealous. They love you but don't try to screw up your head.

BIANCA JAGGER

———

I'm not homosexual, but I certainly understand it's an alternative lifestyle. What's wrong with that?

Actor JOHN FORSYTHE

———

The only thing I want to know is whether a person is kind or unkind.

Actress BUTTERFLY McQUEEN,
asked her opinion of gay rights

———

Robin Tyler: She's had enough of religion made simple-minded.

The most gentle people in the world are macho males, people who are confident in their masculinity and have a feeling of well-being in themselves. They don't have to kick in doors, mistreat women or make fun of gays.

CLINT EASTWOOD

I am deeply, deeply, deeply prejudiced against homosexuality...

Former U.S. Senator S.I. HAYAKAWA (R-California)

Do you remember a time when the word "gay" had a pleasant meaning to it? Why, "gay" is a Bible word. Everybody's happy and gay, the song says ... Christmas songs talk about being adorned with gay apparel, God forbid! I'm so turned off by the word "gay," I won't even use Ben-Gay. Plain old Mentholatum'll do now.

Dallas evangelist JAMES ROBISON

To me, they're not gays, they're fruits.

JAMES GRIFFIN, mayor of Buffalo, New York

The other day a big, tall, blond, nice-looking fellow came up to me and said, "Gee, Michael, I think you're wonderful. I sure would like to go to bed with you." I looked at him and said, "When's the last time you read the Bible? You know you really should read it because there is some information in there about homosexuality." The guy says, "I guess if I'd been a girl, it would have been different." And I said, "No, there are some very direct words on *that* in the Bible too."

MICHAEL JACKSON

Michael Jackson's organization keeps telling everybody he's not a homosexual. You get the feeling something's going on there.

BOY GEORGE

I'm an alcoholic. I'm a drug addict. I'm homosexual. I'm a genius. Of course, I could be all four of these dubious things and still be a saint.

TRUMAN CAPOTE

"Well," said one reporter, "if you don't like the publicity, why don't you go away and change your name?" I replied, "I've just been away, and I have just changed my name. What more do you want me to do?"

Transsexual CHRISTINE JORGENSEN; Jorgensen made world headlines in 1953 after having undergone the first well-publicized, successful sex-change operation; asked once, in 1978, if she ever had any contact with other famous transsexuals, such as tennis player Renee Richards, Jorgensen replied, "People ask me that and I say, 'Listen. You know, we don't have a convention of transsexuals.' I'm not going to call up and say, 'Hi Renee — you'll never guess who this is.' We're not exactly like the Shriners."

Reclusive? I'm not reclusive. I'm a guy that dances on tables, puts lampshades on his head, sticks his dick out in crowds.

MEL GIBSON

Since beauty is unrelated to function, a good-looking man is a luxury from a sexual point of view.

Poet W.H. AUDEN (1907-1973)

Crucifixes are sexy because there's a naked man on them.

Pop star MADONNA

My interest in men is stronger than ever. I have a double-thyroid, ya know . . . It means I have twice as much sexual vitality. That sort of thing runs in the family. My father was a boxer and my mother was famed far and near for her hourglass figure — she

Mae West: The double-thyroid is the secret.

was New York's top corset model at one time. And one of my grandmothers had three breasts!

MAE WEST, in her eighties

―――――

Here lies David Diamond — underneath Tom Cruise.

Openly gay rock musician DAVE DIAMOND, of the group "Berlin," asked what he would most like his epitaph to read

―――――

In the charming season of the flower-time of youth, thou shalt love boys, yearning for their thighs and honeyed mouth.

Athenian statesman and poet SOLON (639-559 B.C.)

―――――

A thing of beauty is a boy forever.

Novelist and critic CARL VAN VECHTEN (1880-1964)

I had the experience with *The Joy of Gay Sex*, when it was being distributed in Canada, that a woman thought she was buying *The Joy of Cooking*. She went home and looked up "chicken" and was absolutely appalled. She created a tremendous fuss. . .

EDMUND WHITE

———

You know, homosexuality is a worldwide economic fact. In poor countries — like Morocco and parts of Italy — it's one of the big industries, one of the main ways in which a young boy can get somewhere.

WILLIAM S. BURROUGHS

———

Don't accept candy from strangers: get real estate.

*GRAFFITI in the bathroom of a hustlers' bar
in New York City*

———

If it be sin to love a lovely lad,
Oh then sin I.

*English poet RICHARD BARNFIELD
(1574-1627),* The Affectionate Shepherd,
1594

———

I can't imagine having an affair with someone to whom I have to explain what I'm doing.

QUENTIN CRISP, on boy-love

———

The song is about . . . Quentin Crisp. I think he is one of the most courageous men I've ever met, and one of the wittiest. He was flamboyantly gay at a time when it was physically dangerous to be gay. He lives near the Bowery, and he has an unbelievable sense of humor and joy in life that everybody can draw a lesson from. It was my song to appreciate his singularity.

*STING, discussing his 1987 song
"Englishman in New York"; the song's refrain
is, "Be yourself, no matter what they say."*

Undoubtedly it is difficult for anyone to understand or believe that a boy, a man who suspects himself to be homosexual, can practice lifelong self-deception, can actually convince himself that a major element of his personality is simply untrue. It can be and is done hundreds of thousands of times each day. Someone recently referred to me as "an admitted homosexual," but that was not an accurate description during most of my life. I admitted nothing, especially to myself.

> *Former Congressman ROBERT BAUMAN*
> *(R-Maryland); while still a congressman,*
> *Bauman was arrested for soliciting sex with a*
> *teenage boy. Shortly afterward, his wife had*
> *their twenty-one-year marriage annulled, and his*
> *political career came to an end*

———

I've only once in my whole career ever had a person stand up in the audience and ask me if I was gay. And it was a guy in Florida, and I said, "Why? Have you fallen hopelessly in love with me?" And the guy just fled the room.

> *Novelist REYNOLDS PRICE*

———

I tried to persuade myself that I was three-quarters normal and that only a quarter of me was queer — whereas really it was the other way round.

> *W. SOMERSET MAUGHAM*

———

I mean look at Tchaikovsky. His music is absolutely hysterical because he had to hide the fact that he was a homosexual ... Well this obviously comes out in his music, great music, but music of suffering, pain and torment, and this very placid-looking gentleman who smiles out of his benign beard from these faded photographs is a mask for the torment that you can see and feel in his music ... Of course the Russians still don't admit that he *was* a homosexual. I've been over his house, I've talked to the guides there, and as soon as you mention it they just pretty well frog-march you to the door.

> *KEN RUSSELL, director of* The
> Music Lovers, *a 1971 film biography of*

Tchaikovsky, starring Richard Chamberlain and Glenda Jackson

———

It is better to be hated for what one is than loved for what one is not.

French writer ANDRE GIDE (1869-1951)

———

I remember one time I scratched this girl's back in the middle of the night — I was, you know, nine, and she was twelve, and she asked me to scratch her back. A nun ran in, ripped me off her back, threw me against the lockers, beat the shit out of me and called me a lesbian. I didn't know what a lesbian was.

Pop star CYNDI LAUPER, on her experiences in a Catholic boarding school

———

Straights can learn a lot from us gay people. We teach straight people so many things about sexuality. Like, perhaps, not to take it quite so seriously . . . not to kill each other over it.

ARMISTEAD MAUPIN

———

The first time I saw a film of mine, I laughed all the way through it.

Porn star RICHARD LOCKE

———

When I was young, homosexuality was a forbidden fruit, something special, a fruit to be gathered with care, not what it is today — hundreds of homosexuals showing off, dancing together in a gay bar.

Italian film director LUCHINO VISCONTI (1906-1976)

———

Gay liberation should not be a license to be a perpetual adolescent. If you deny yourself commitment then what can you do with your life?

HARVEY FIERSTEIN

The life of a homosexual is lonely in its passing contacts and in its progenitive barrenness...

JOHN UPDIKE

Gentlemen don't prefer blondes. If I were writing that book today, I'd call it *Gentlemen Prefer Gentlemen.*

Playwright and novelist ANITA LOOS (1893-1981), author of Gentlemen Prefer Blondes

---

It seems like soon it will be weird to be heterosexual.

Harvard coed, quoted in a 1982 Newsweek *article on gay rights*

After I had introduced legislation into the Texas House of Representatives to ban homosexual groups from our college campuses, the head man at Texas A&M came to me frantic and nervous and said, "Clay, please keep pushing. We ain't even used to girls yet."

Former Texas State Representative CLAY SMOTHERS (R)

Queers shouldn't be allowed to use public property.

Former Lieutenant Governor of Nevada MYRON LEAVITT, on the National Gay Rodeo's use of the Nevada State Fairgrounds in Reno

---

You could move.

ABIGAIL VAN BUREN ("Dear Abby"), in response to a homophobic reader who launched into a bitter tirade against gay men moving into a house across the street and then asked, "How can we improve the quality of the ... neighborhood?"

The church thought we were sinful. The health field took us as sick. The capitalist saw us as unemployable and the nuclear family mistook us for a birth defect.

Veteran gay activist MORRIS KIGHT

———

Straight people don't care about us. They really don't. And if we don't take care of ourselves, we're going to be in even more trouble than we already are.

COLT THOMAS,
"Mr. International Leather" 1983

———

Bring me your tired old queens, your poor drags,
Your horny masses yearning to be free,
The disco bunnies of this teeming land,
Send me these tempest-toss'd homos,
And I will lift my skirts and take them in.

Writer GREG JACKSON's proposed re-
wording of the Emma Lazarus poem at the base
of the Statue of Liberty

———

We'll take almost anything. I am waiting for some leatherman to send us a motorcycle with a used slave on it.

JOHN HAMMOND, co-founder of the
International Gay History Archives

———

There's a lot of talk these days about homosexuals coming out of the closet. I didn't know they'd been in the closet. I do know they've always been in the gutter.

JERRY FALWELL

———

We are all in the gutter, but some of us are looking at the stars.

OSCAR WILDE (1854-1900)

GROWING UP GAY

I'm everything you were afraid your little girl would grow up to be
— and your little boy.

> BETTE MIDLER

———

I wasn't the most masculine child. The words "sissy" and "let's get
him" were familiar to my ears . . . Up in my room, I put on my
own Broadway routines. I was the only person I knew who
danced to the *I Love Lucy* theme.

> Openly gay comic TERRY SWEENEY,
> famous for his impersonations of First Lady
> Nancy Reagan on Saturday Night Live

———

I was *always* fascinated by glamour. Compared to watching Joan
Crawford sweep down staircases, making mud pies was really a
bore.

> Novelist RICHARD FRIEDEL,
> author of The Movie Lover

———

. . . the boy who, at fourteen or fifteen is still deeply interested in
cutting out paper dolls or embroidering initials on his pocket
handkerchiefs; or the girl who, after the menstrual cycle has been
definitely established, still gets a thrill out of swinging a pick and

Bette Midler: Everything you were afraid your little boy would grow up to be.

shovel, or carrying fifty-pound stones around to build a wall with, will bear watching.

> *DR. LA FOREST POTTER, in his 1933 book on homosexuality,* Strange Loves

———

Sweating is good for a boy and will help him avoid homosexual tendencies.

> *Baptist minister JACK HYLES, in a 1982 pamphlet entitled "Jesus Had Short Hair"*

———

If I had a son and he was watching some guy making music on television, and he came downstairs with makeup on and his mother's shoes and said I want to be like so-and-so, I'd beat the shit out of him . . . I want my boys to wear men's clothes and my daughters to wear women's.

> *EDDIE MURPHY, in a 1985 interview in* Cosmopolitan

I was eight years old and she came to the Easter Egg Roll wearing jodphurs and riding boots. I'm *sure* that had an influence on my life. . .

SALLY GEARHART, on meeting and
shaking hands with former First Lady Eleanor
Roosevelt

He was a very good, but very strange boy.

LOUISA WHITMAN, recalling the childhood
of her son Walt Whitman (1819-1892)

I thought he was trying to shock me — that was the kind of boy he was. But then I saw that he was serious. He was even wondering if he should move out of the house. I told him not to worry about my reaction. He was still my son.

JERRY O'DOWD, Boy George's father,
recalling when Boy George was fifteen and
announced to his father he thought he was gay

Sure. I told them when I was sixteen . . . I had a boyfriend in high school. They *freaked*. You know, all the usual bullshit, "How could you choose this kind of lifestyle, Peter?" I said, "Hey, guys, it chose me." I mean, your dick knows what it likes. When you reach puberty you don't fuckin' decide what sex you like; you ask your dick. You say, "Hey, dick, what do you like?" Okay. All right. Then you go for it.

Peter, on telling his parents he was gay,
in BILL SHERWOOD's 1986 film,
Parting Glances

You see, I am a homosexual. I have fought it off for months and maybe years, but it just grows truer.

A teenage son to his mother, in LAURA Z.
HOBSON's novel Consenting Adult, *1975*

. . .surely homosexuality is an injury to healthy functioning, a distortion of personality. And the grounds for believing that it is a socially acquired inclination are reasons for prudence. To the extent that homosexuality is, in some sense, a "choice" . . . then that choice may be influenced by various things, including a social atmosphere of indifference or sustained exposure to homosexual role models, such as teachers.

Conservative columnist GEORGE WILL, during the 1977 battle over gay rights in Dade County, Florida

There is no need for parents to fear homosexual teachers. Ninety-seven percent of child seduction is heterosexual.

DR. BENJAMIN SPOCK

I can't imagine teachers having any influence on whether students become homosexual or heterosexual. Anita Bryant's ideas about homosexual teachers recruiting young boys is nonsense. It goes against all the facts we have.

Sex researcher DR. WARDELL POMEROY

It's not contagious. I didn't catch it.

LARRY KING, husband of tennis pro Billie Jean King, interviewed after his wife publicly acknowledged that she had had a lesbian affair

I am interested in recruiting teenagers. I am interested in recruiting every gay teenager who is out there. I want him to know he is gay. I want him to be proud of it as soon as possible, as early as possible, because of all the pain and suffering that kids go through that makes their lives fucked up from then on. I think a teenager can know and be aware of his sexuality when he is thirteen.

TOM REEVES, spokesman for the radical boy-love movement

To me, realizing I was gay was almost like being told I had cancer at the time. I thought, "My God, here I am slipping away from

Aaron Fricke: A rock lobster comes out of his shell.

my family, my society; I'm going to be invisible." I felt a physical sensation of being on a ship, and the ship was leaving from the dock and everyone was standing on the dock and the ship was moving, and I could do nothing to get off that ship, and the stretch of water was getting wider and wider between us.

Writer ANDREW HOLLERAN

———

Even now I can only vaguely realize that it was only comparatively late in life that I would go into a room full of people without a feeling of guilt. To go into a room full of men, or to a lavatory in the Savoy, needed quite an effort. With success in my work this situation became easier ... but to feel that one was not a felon and an outcast could have helped enormously during the difficult young years.

Photographer and designer CECIL BEATON
(1904-1980)

...when I grew up we had no positive images if we were gay. I was totally lost — I was just this fat faggot living out in Brooklyn. All I knew about gays was that they always got beaten up in some Philip Marlowe movie.

HARVEY FIERSTEIN

———

I became not merely a self-confessed homosexual, but a self-evident one. That is to say I put my case not only before the people who knew me but also before strangers. This was not difficult to do. I wore makeup at a time when even on women eye shadow was sinful ... From that moment on, my friends were anyone who could put up with the disgrace ... To survive at all was an adventure; to reach old age was a miracle.

QUENTIN CRISP,
The Naked Civil Servant, *1978*

———

The simple, obvious thing would have been to go to the senior prom with a girl. But that would have been a lie — a lie to myself, to the girl, and to all the other students. What I wanted to do was to take a male date. But ... such honesty is not always easy.

AARON FRICKE, in his book Reflections of a Rock Lobster; *Fricke made national headlines when he sued his high school for the right to take a male date to the senior prom in 1980.*

———

I was expecting more trouble than we got. Mostly the guys just jeered and called us fag and queer — that sort of thing.

PAUL GUILBERT, Aaron Fricke's date at the senior prom

———

I have to admit that basically, I am gay. Homosexuals go through a lot of pain, and I would support anyone who is totally frank, because it's not ever easy. My mother was the first person I told that I was gay. She was understanding, and still is. That made it easier for me. I've always had a good relationship with her.

ELTON JOHN, in a 1983 interview

"I suppose I should be upset," he told me, "but as long as you're a faggot, you might as well be a famous faggot." I thought it was extraordinarily tolerant on his part.

ARMISTEAD MAUPIN, on his father's reaction when he found out, from an article in Newsweek, *that Armistead was gay*

My father, who is sixty-six, thinks my success is great. When he found out I was making money, he wanted to become involved in my enterprise! He's a jock; he's at the Y all day playing handball. Several years ago, he happened to walk into an adult bookstore; on the way to the hetero section, he happened to see my face on the cover of a gay magazine ... and needless to say he was quite surprised. He not only learned that I was a star, but he learned at the same time that I'm gay. It didn't bother him in the least.

Porn star AL PARKER

I had hated it for years ... For twelve years his secret, of course, had been my secret ... In public I had laughed at jokes about homosexuals, fearful that angry protest might "give something away." When somebody would ask, "And your other son — is he married?" I would offhandedly say, "Still playing the field, I guess."

LAURA Z. HOBSON (1900-1986), author of Consenting Adult; *Hobson's son Christopher had told her he was gay when he was seventeen.*

There are some things a mother has a right not to know.

A mother to her son, as he tried to tell her he was gay, in ANDREW HOLLERAN's novel Nights in Aruba, *1983*

I know somebody who is Jewish and homosexual. His parents told him, "We *know*. We know the life you lead. But you *must* marry. After that, you can carry on whatever way you want." I consider that the most awful piece of family advice I've ever heard. Of course, they're an American family, and Americans seem to have more hang-ups about these things than the Europeans do.

JOHN SCHLESINGER,
director of Midnight Cowboy
and Sunday, Bloody Sunday

———

We do not need the homosexual, they need us. Unless they live natural like us, they cannot and will not survive. God's truth is our shield and we can rest in peace and assurance that the homosexual is on his way out, unless he does as we do. Isn't it wonderful how God has provided us protection from them? They cannot produce unless they live as we do. We are and shall ever be in control.

LETTER TO THE EDITOR, in a
Colorado newspaper, 1981

———

You will never be rid of us because we produce ourselves out of your bodies.

Writer MARTHA SHELLEY

———

We conclude that being a gay male is a familial trait. It isn't just randomly distributed.

DR. RICHARD C. PILLARD, co-author of
a 1986 Boston University School of Medicine
study that found that gay men are five times
more likely than heterosexual men to have a gay
brother

———

An old guy I know believes that nature created homosexuality as an alternative to war as a means of controlling the population. It's very idealistic, but I don't agree with it. Homosexuality has always been around. It's just more visible now. You can't pretend it doesn't exist anymore.

BOY GEORGE

———

Fairies: Nature's attempt to get rid of soft boys by sterilizing them.

F. SCOTT FITZGERALD (1896-1940)

You mentioned that men may be shying away from heterosexuality because women are becoming more sexually demanding — and I certainly think that's true. I have no doubt that some men turn to homosexuality because they just cannot face the pressure.

HELEN GURLEY BROWN,
editor of Cosmopolitan

I certainly wasn't real confident with girls. I guess that's what got me started with guys. And small animals.

Actor JON-ERIK HEXUM (1957-1984)

I grew up thinking that women didn't have assholes because they were too pure to shit. I never heard my mother fart and never smelled anything ... My mother led me to believe that men were dirty because they always wanted sex and that women were always clean and kept themselves washed all the time the way she did. As a result men became very interesting to me...

Poet ROBERT PETERS

I have been perfectly happy the way I am. If my mother was responsible for it, I am grateful.

CHRISTOPHER ISHERWOOD

All homosexuals are philosophers. Which is a fact I've sometimes discovered to my dismay when I've dragged home An Innocent Farm Boy or A Menacing Motorcyclist and prepared myself to dive into a fantasy. Hopefully, the fantasy may last through the sex, but afterward I invariably detect beneath the innocence or the menace a detached, analytic, self-conscious turn of mind ... for every homosexual, whether he be a truck driver or a defense attorney, has at least one big theory, one theory he's forever building, modulating, extending, scrapping or revising: Why am I gay?

EDMUND WHITE

I don't have any theory about homosexuality. I don't even have a theory about undifferentiated desire. I ascertain that I'm homosexual. OK. That's no cause for alarm. How and why are idle questions. It's a little like my wanting to know why my eyes are green.

French writer JEAN GENET (1910-1986)

———

How can it be that a vice, one which would destroy the human race if it became general, an infamous assault upon nature, can nevertheless be so natural? It looks like the last degree of thought-out corruption, and at the same time, it is the usual possession of those who haven't had time to be corrupted yet. It has entered hearts still new, that haven't known either ambition, nor fraud, nor the thirst of riches...

VOLTAIRE (1694-1778),
Philosophical Dictionary, *1764*

———

The "adults only" world of sex appealed to me almost as far back as I can remember ... Some boys grow up dreaming about becoming astronauts. I grew up dreaming about hustling — of being used for sex. This was one of my regular fantasies.

Porn star ROY GARRETT

———

I was a love-starved, fresh-faced, innocent, blooming virgin, starry-eyed with romantic idealism, who masturbated six or seven times a day and grew more introverted and unhappy as no outlet for my love materialized. All I wanted was just *one* boy my own age. I had all kinds of crushes ... I remember many of them now; even their names bring back some of those first pangs of puppy-love, hero-worship: William Gilmore, Nick Gaponovitch, Irving Brodsky, Joe di Bona. They're as alive for me now as they were then.

HAROLD NORSE

———

Between the ages of ten and twenty-four, my only lover was my right hand ... I had no idea there were men out there who liked to fuck men.

RICHARD LOCKE

The first love of anyone's life is usually a powerful conditioning factor. In my case I was fortunate to experience at the school a remarkable, an ineffable love relationship which lasted until I was fifteen. He was not the first boy I had been to bed with, but he was certainly the most ravishing ... He was captain of the baseball team, muscular, blond, with one of the most beautiful penises I have ever known intimately. Furthermore he possessed an absolutely intoxicating body odor ... He taught me the raptures of sexuality.

> *Poet JAMES BROUGHTON*

For I cannot say what is a greater good for a man in his youth than a lover, and for a lover than a beloved. For that which ought to guide mankind through all his life, if it is to be a good life, noble blood cannot implant in him so well, nor office, nor wealth, nor anything but Love.

> *From the speech of Phaidros, in PLATO's* Symposium *(c. 384 B.C.)*

I was perhaps eight, not more than ten years old, very young in any case, out in the country in the Mettray reformatory where homosexuality was not, of course, approved of; but since there weren't any girls there, it was unavoidable for all the boys between fifteen and twenty-one; there wasn't any recourse but transitory homosexuality or permanent homosexuality, but in any case, to homosexuality, and that's what makes it possible for me to say that I was really happy in the reformatory.

> *JEAN GENET*

The first time I had sex with another man was ... in Portugal right after the revolution in that country in 1974. I met an eighteen-year-old French Canadian boy in Lisbon who was on his way to Afghanistan. We began to travel together, and became very close. In the post-revolutionary atmosphere of a euphoric Portugal, we allowed ourselves that final break with traditional morality. We spent a month together making love on the windy beaches at night before it was time to go our separate ways. I was heartbroken when it was time to part.

Model and photographer KRISTEN BJORN

———

I think I was twenty-five the first time I had sex. I stopped at twenty-six.

ANDY WARHOL (1927-1987)

———

It was only at eighteen that I was finally liberated sexually. My way always was only with boys. With them I discovered the full delights of sex.

ROGER PEYREFITTE

———

When I was about seventeen, eighteen, at that time I took the sewing machine of my grandmother and started to take in my pants — because I always felt they didn't show the body like they should . . . You could buy tight pants at the time, but they never showed crotch, and that was for me — and still is — the nicest part of the body.

Porn star PETER BERLIN

———

A handsome son keeps his parents in constant fear and misery; so rarely do modesty and good looks go together.

Roman satirist JUVENAL (A.D. 65-128)

———

Lord, give me chastity . . . but not yet!

ST. AUGUSTINE (354-430), in his youth

SWEET INTERCOURSE

The debating society at my school was discussing the motion "That the present generation has lost the ability to entertain itself." Rising to make my maiden speech, I said with shaky aplomb, "Mr. Chairman — as long as masturbation exists, no one can seriously maintain that we have lost the ability to entertain ourselves." The teacher in charge immediately closed the meeting.

Theater critic KENNETH TYNAN
(1927-1980)

———

A married lady who is a leader in the social purity movements and an enthusiast for sexual chastity, discovered through reading some pamphlets against solitary vice that she herself had been practicing masturbation for years without knowing it. The profound anguish and hopeless despair of this woman in the face of what she believed to be the moral ruin of her whole life cannot well be described.

English psychologist and sex researcher
HAVELOCK ELLIS (1859-1939)

———

As an amusement it is too fleeting. As an occupation it is too wearing. As a public exhibition there is no money in it. It is unsuited to the drawing room.

MARK TWAIN (1835-1910),
on masturbation

What you are losing between your fingers, Ponticus, is a human being!

> Roman poet *MARTIAL (A.D. 40-104)*,
> *in an epigram on masturbation*

Most homosexuals find their man-to-man sex unfulfilling so they masturbate a lot ... Carrots and cucumbers are pressed into service ... Sometimes the whole egg in the shell finds itself where it doesn't belong. Sausages, especially the milder varieties, are popular. The homosexual who prefers to use his penis must find an anus. Many look in the refrigerator. The most common masturbatory object for this purpose is a melon. Cantaloupes are usual, but where it is available, papaya is popular.

> *DR. DAVID REUBEN, in his misnamed*
> Everything You Always Wanted to Know
> About Sex, But Were Afraid to Ask, *1969*

Mark Twain: He didn't really dislike it, he just wanted to keep a good thing secret.

I can get an erection by just thinking or by looking at myself . . . I make people come in their pants who have never done it.

PETER BERLIN

To love oneself is the beginning of a lifelong romance.

OSCAR WILDE

Sex is everything in life. The trees, the flowers, everything exists through sex. Some people are born one way, others another. I adore my sexual experiences. They are the most thrilling moments of my life, and if I were castrated there would be no future interest . . . to live for.

British writer BEVERLEY NICHOLS (1898-1983)

When you are as old as I, young man, you will know there is only one thing in the world worth living for, and that is sin.

LADY SPERANZA WILDE (1821-1896), mother of Oscar Wilde, when she was in her sixties

[E.M. Forster] said to me that when he was a young man all he thought about was sex. He was obsessed by sex and he kept thinking, "How wonderful it will be when I'm forty and I'll have eased up on all of this." And when he was forty it got worse. He thought, "My gosh, when I get to be fifty I'll have some relief." At fifty it was worse and he said, "Surely by the time I'm sixty..." Then suddenly he was seventy and seventy-five and he said, "I'm seventy-five years old and it's worse than it ever was. I'm finding myself thinking about it continuously now that I can hardly do anything about it."

TRUMAN CAPOTE

Sophocles said at eighty, "I am at last free of a cruel and insane master." Well, I've thirty-one years to go.

GORE VIDAL, asked, when he was forty-nine, if he still had a keen sexual appetite

To the young, sex is what grown-ups do. To the elderly, sex is what the young do.

NED ROREM

———

I am convinced that happy, guiltless, and lusty intercourse stimulates the circulation and digestion, gets all the glands going, and is the best physical medicine in the world. Although some of my best friends are men, and homosexual men at that, my preference is to do this with women. But that is my own taste, and it would never occur to me to impose it on others...

Writer and philosopher ALAN WATTS
(1915-1973)

———

Most of my male friends are gay, and that seems perfectly natural to me. I mean, who wouldn't like cock?

Actress VALERIE PERRINE

———

A healthy sex life. Best thing in the world for a woman's voice.

Soprano LEONTYNE PRICE

———

Sexual union is the most religious experience possible, it is the most thrilling form of meditation, it is direct contact with the divine ... I have always thought that a solution for the ills of the world would be to send all boys to a school that taught them to love one another. And I mean real loving ... I don't mean rhetorical peptalks. I mean get them all into bed together to learn the ecstatic habit of male love.

JAMES BROUGHTON

———

The world seems more cheerful if, when we wake up in the morning, we find we are no longer alone and that there is another human being beside us in the half-dark. That's more cheerful than shelves of edifying books and the whitewashed walls of a church...

VINCENT VAN GOGH (1853-1890)

Actress Valerie Perrine: A penchant for the best things in life.

The art of life lies in taking pleasures as they pass, and the keenest pleasures are not intellectual, nor are they always moral.
Greek philosopher ARISTIPPUS
(435-366 B.C.)

No civilized man ever regrets a pleasure, and no uncivilized man ever knows what a pleasure is.
OSCAR WILDE

A very good-looking boy followed me for a quarter of an hour, and in the end he came up to me outside the Opera ... I went back with him to his home and he kissed me with a frenzy even on the staircase ... I was wildly passionate ... We made love like tigers until dawn...

> *Silent screen star RUDOLPH VALENTINO*
> *(1895-1926), in an entry in his private journal*

———

After Mohammed had left me, I spent a long time in a state of quivering jubiliation, and although I had already achieved pleasure five times with him, I revived my ecstacy over and over again, and back in my hotel room, prolonged the echoes of it until morning.

> *ANDRE GIDE, on an evening spent in*
> *Algiers with a young musician, Mohammed,*
> *when Gide was twenty-four*

———

So we had sex, or at least I lay and allowed him to fuck me, and thought as his prick shot in and he kissed my neck, back and shoulders, that it was a most unappetising position for a world-famous artist to be in.

> *JOE ORTON, in his diary, after having sex*
> *with an eighteen-year-old Moroccan boy*

———

It's such fun being mauled slightly by some quite strange person with whom one has nothing in common.

> *CECIL BEATON*

———

In the frenzied pursuit of the object of one's affection, human beings are almost always at their antic worst. Two squirts of adrenalin and we're off and running, all reason and good sense thrown as caution to the wind. The lengths to which we will go in making fools of ourselves for just a simple roll in the hay are known intimately to each of us.

> *MARTIN GREIF*

———

To me, passionate love has always been like a tight shoe rubbing blisters on my Achilles heel ... I resent and love it and wallow

... and I wish to God I could handle it but I never have and I know I never will.

NOEL COWARD (1899-1973), when he
was fifty-eight and became infatuated with a
young man half his age

———

When you meet a boy who pleases you, take action at once. Don't be polite — just grab him by the balls and strike while the iron is hot.

ADDAEUS OF MACEDONIA
(c. A.D. 1st century)

———

I can also defend, on what appears to me sufficient grounds, a large amount of promiscuity. In the very nature of the sexual contact between two males there inheres an element of instability. No children come of the connection. There can be no marriage ceremonies, no marriage settlements, no married life in common. Therefore, the parties are free, and the sexual flower of comradeship may spring afresh for each of them wherever favourable soil is found.

JOHN ADDINGTON SYMONDS,
in his memoirs, 1890

———

The main thing is that the act male homosexuals commit is ugly and repugnant and afterwards they are disgusted with themselves. They drink and take drugs, to palliate this, but they are disgusted with the act and they are always changing partners and cannot be really happy. In women it is the opposite. They do nothing that they are disgusted by and nothing that is repulsive and afterwards they are happy and they can lead happy lives together.

GERTRUDE STEIN (1874-1946),
as quoted by Ernest Hemingway in
A Moveable Feast

———

The homosexual must constantly search for the one man, the one penis, the one experience that will satisfy him. Tragically there is no possibility of satisfaction . . . Disappointed, stubborn, discouraged, defiant, the homosexual keeps trying. He is the sexual Diogenes, always looking for the penis that pleases. That is the reason he must change partners endlessly.

> DR. DAVID REUBEN, Everything You
> Always Wanted to Know About Sex, But
> Were Afraid to Ask, *1969*

———

. . . the heterosexual male's obsession with cock is far beyond that of any fag. I remember recently reading about a college where the black boys and the white boys were living in the same dormitory. The black boys asked to move out. When the whites asked why, the blacks said, "Because these white cats are always looking at our cocks. That's all they think about is cock. We're not into that."

> GORE VIDAL

———

Honey, I was wondering, um — do you have two of anything *else*?

> Line from the 1972 horror film The Thing
> With Two Heads

———

I do not find male genitals particularly attractive. They look like coconuts hanging off a tree. Or as the elephant said to the naked man, "How the hell do you breathe through that?"

> Television actor DUNCAN REGEHR

———

The act of coitus and the members that serve it are so hideous that if it were not for . . . the liberation of the soul, the human species would lose its humanity.

> LEONARDO DA VINCI (1452-1519)

———

Listen, Tommy, I'll take care of the music. You just stick to sucking cock!

> Soprano EILEEN FARRELL, to gay
> conductor Thomas Schippers (1930-1977),
> after Schippers reprimanded her during a
> rehearsal at the Metropolitan Opera

There are times I wish I had a bigger cock. We all have that. I imagine John Holmes at times would wish to have a bigger cock, although God knows why.

RICHARD LOCKE

———

I'm not sure, but perhaps I can *initial* it.

TENNESSEE WILLIAMS, to a homophobic drunk who whipped out his limp penis in a restaurant one night and snidely asked Williams to autograph it (Truman Capote also laid claim to this retort)

———

If discovering you're gay means finding yourself considered the scum of the earth, then discovering that you enjoy S/M means learning that you're thought to be the devil incarnate. It is no picnic being thought weird, especially by those whom everyone else calls perverted.

Writer ARNIE KANTROWITZ

———

People tend to think of sadomasochism as anything but controlled, conjuring up visions of screaming victims desperately anxious to escape the clutches of tormentors whose passions drive them on to more and more dangerous abuses. If this were true, few people would acquire a taste for S/M sex and those who did would not survive long. Common sense would suggest that people do what they do sexually, not out of perversity, but because they actually find pleasure in it.

PETER FISHER,
The Gay Mystique, *1972*

———

Many people who aren't into S/M feel that hate is the force behind it . . . But it's not that. It's an understanding between two people of what each wants. It's pleasure, no matter how it looks to others, and to share pleasure with another person is love.

Artist TOM OF FINLAND

Fool — don't put him in irons; put him in the infantry.
> *FREDERICK THE GREAT, upon being*
> *informed that a soldier had been fettered in irons*
> *for committing bestiality with his horse*

———

The only unnatural sex act is that which you cannot perform.
> *Pioneering sex researcher*
> *DR. ALFRED KINSEY (1894-1956)*

———

A happy property of sexual acts, and perhaps especially of homo-sexual acts, is that they are dirty, like life ... In a society as middle-class, orderly, and technological as ours, it is essential to break down squeamishness, which is an important factor in what is called racism, as well as in cruelty to children and the sterile putting away of the sick and aged.
> *Writer and social activist PAUL GOODMAN*
> *(1911-1972)*

———

Chastity is the most unnatural of all the sexual perversions.
> *French critic REMY DE GOURMONT*
> *(1858-1915)*

OSCAR WILDE

If a man gets drunk, whether he does so on white wine or red is of no importance. If a man has perverse passions, their particular mode of manifestation is of no importance either.

OSCAR WILDE

Oscar was not a man of bad character: you could have trusted him with a woman anywhere.

WILLIE WILDE (1852-1899),
Oscar Wilde's brother

It is hateful to me now to speak or write of such things, but I must be explicit. Sodomy never took place between us, nor was it thought or dreamt of. Wilde treated me as an older boy treats a younger one at school, and he added what was new to me and was not (as far as I know) known or practised among my contemporaries: he "sucked" me.

LORD ALFRED DOUGLAS (1870-1945),
clarifying his sexual relationship with Oscar
Wilde, in a letter to one of Wilde's biographers

I kissed each one of them in every part of their bodies; they were all dirty and appealed to me just for that reason.

OSCAR WILDE, boasting to a friend of hav-
ing had sexual relations with five young men —

72

all of them telegraph and district messenger boys
— in one night

———

I was asked by Wilde to imagine that I was a woman and that he was my lover. I had to keep up this illusion. I used to sit on his knees and he used to play with my privates as a man might amuse himself with a girl.

Young male prostitute, testifying for the prosecution at Wilde's trial, in 1895, on charges of having committed indecent acts

———

I am the Love that dare not speak its name.

LORD ALFRED DOUGLAS, in a poem, "The Two Loves," 1892; this was the first appearance of the famous phrase

———

"The Love that dare not speak its name" in this century is such a great affection of an elder for a younger man as there was between David and Jonathan, such as Plato made the very basis of his philosophy, and such as you find in the sonnets of Michelangelo and Shakespeare. It is that deep, spiritual affection that is as pure as it is perfect. It dictates and pervades great works of art like those of Shakespeare and Michelangelo, and those two letters of mine, such as they are. It is in this century misunderstood, so much misunderstood that it may be described as "the Love that dare not speak its name," and on account of it I am placed where I am now. It is beautiful, it is fine, it is the noblest form of affection. There is nothing unnatural about it. It is intellectual, and it repeatedly exists between an elder and a younger man, where the elder has intellect and the younger has all the joy, hope, and glamor of life before him. That it should be so, the world does not understand. The world mocks at it and sometimes puts one in the pillory for it.

Testimony made by OSCAR WILDE at his trial; Wilde's remarks drew a loud response of applause, as well as some hisses, from the spectators' gallery

Oscar Wilde . . . the crime of which you have been convicted is so bad that one has to put stern restraint upon one's self to prevent one's self from describing, in language which I would rather not use, the sentiments that must rise to the breast of every man of honour who has heard the details of these two terrible trials . . . It is no use for me to address you. People who can do these things must be dead to all sense of shame . . . It is the worst case I have ever tried.

> SIR ALFRED WILLS, presiding judge at Wilde's trial, in remarks before sentencing Wilde to two years' hard labor in prison

---

My God, my God! And I? May I say nothing, my lord?

> OSCAR WILDE, upon hearing the Court's sentence; according to witnesses, Wilde's face blanched with anguish when he heard the sentence, and despite his pleas to speak, the judge motioned for him to be removed from the courtroom.

He'll have his hair cut reg'lar now!

> Female prostitute outside the courthouse, after hearing the terms of Wilde's sentence; her remark provoked general laughter among other spectators.

No sterner rebuke could well have been inflicted on some of the artistic tendencies of the time than the condemnation of Oscar Wilde at the Central Criminal Court. Young men at the universities, silly women who lend an ear to idle chatter which is petulant and vicious, novelists who have sought to imitate the style of paradox and unreality, poets who have lisped the language of nerveless and effeminate libertinage — these are the persons who should ponder with themselves the doctrine and career of the man who has now to undergo the righteous sentence of the law.

> Editorial in the London DAILY TELEGRAPH the morning after Wilde was sentenced to prison

For many years, both in England and in America, the Wilde scandal had a disastrous influence, not upon writers and artists themselves but upon the attitude of the general public toward the arts, since it allowed the philistine man to identify himself with the decent man. Though the feeling that it is sissy for a boy to take an interest in the arts has probably always existed among the middle class and is not yet extinct, for many years after Wilde's trial it was enormously intensified.

W.H. AUDEN

The public is wonderfully tolerant. It forgives everything except genius.

OSCAR WILDE

If Oscar Wilde, instead of indulging in dirty tricks of indecent familiarity with boys and men, had ruined the lives of half a dozen innocent simpletons of girls, or had broken up the home of his friend by corrupting his friend's wife, no one could have laid a finger upon him. The male is sacrosanct; the female is fair game. To have burdened society with a dozen bastards, to have destroyed a happy home by his lawless lust — of these things the criminal law takes no account. But let him act indecently to a young rascal who is very well able to take care of himself, and who can by no possibility bring a child into the world as the result of his corruption, then judges can hardly contain themselves from indignation when inflicting the maximum sentence the law allows.

London publisher and journalist W. T. STEAD (1849-1912), in one of the only public defenses of Oscar Wilde. Stead's remarks were published shortly after Wilde was sentenced to prison in 1895. As an editor and writer, Stead championed social and military reform during the Victorian era. Tragically, he lost his life on the Titanic *in 1912.*

Frightful bounder. It made me puke to look at him.

> *English aristocrat COLONEL GEORGE*
> *KEPPEL, on Oscar Wilde*

———

I think his fate is rather like Humpty Dumpty's, quite as tragic and quite as impossible to put right.

> *CONSTANCE WILDE (1858-1898), wife*
> *of Oscar Wilde, in a letter to her brother*

———

Our ill-fated and most lamentable friendship has ended in ruin and public infamy for me, yet the memory of our ancient affection is often with me, and the thought that loathing, bitterness and contempt should for ever take that place in my heart once held by love is very sad to me...

> *OSCAR WILDE, in a letter written from*
> *prison to Lord Alfred Douglas in 1897; the*
> *letter was published, under the title* De
> Profundis, *after Wilde's death in 1900.*

———

I have read the Oscar Wilde letters and have come to the reluctant conclusion that he was one of the silliest, most conceited and unattractive characters that ever existed. His love letters to Alfred Lord Douglas are humourless, affected and embarrassing ... *De Profundis* is one long wail of self-pity. It is extraordinary indeed that such a posing, artificial old queen should have written one of the greatest comedies in the English language. In my opinion it was the only thing of the least *importance* that he did write.

> *NOEL COWARD*

———

I admire Wilde's work but not his life, it is an appalling life. Unlike Wilde, I think you should put your genius into your work, not into your life.

> *JOE ORTON*

———

His unhappy fate has done the world a signal service in defeating

Goldie Hawn: A close en-
counter with Oscar Wilde?

the blind obscurantists: he has made people think. Far more people think differently today because of him.

> *English artist and writer LAURENCE*
> *HOUSMAN (1865-1959), on how Wilde's*
> *tragedy, in the long run, influenced many*
> *people's attitudes towards homosexuality and the*
> *law; Laurence, the brother of poet A.E.*
> *Housman, was himself homosexual.*

———

The world is slowly growing more tolerant and one day men will
be ashamed of their barbarous treatment of me, as they are now
ashamed of the torturings of the Middle Ages.

> *OSCAR WILDE, to his friend and biographer*
> *Frank Harris*

And alien tears will fill for him
    Pity's long broken urn,
For his mourners will be outcast men,
    And outcasts always mourn.

Wilde's epitaph, on his tomb in Pere Lachaise
Cemetery in Paris; the lines were taken from
Wilde's work The Ballad of Reading Gaol.

———

Another time, I was in a hotel in Paris, staying in the Oscar Wilde suite. I was sitting with my sister and family, and we were having a glass of champagne and started to laugh about Oscar Wilde's dying in that suite. We were being a little irreverent and — I'll be damned — the bottle, which was half full and sitting firmly on the table, went right over on the counter.

GOLDIE HAWN

———

It was for sinners such as this
Hell was created bottomless.

Poet ALGERNON SWINBURNE
(1837-1909), on Oscar Wilde.

ENTERTAINERS
AND THE ENTERTAINED

I know lots of people who are gay. It's natural to me ... They're the most receptive of any audience I've ever had. They just always seem to have a good time. They seem to be free spirits.
                    DOLLY PARTON

Coming from Jamaica I've always been rather wild and free-spirited. My twin brother was gay and he was really my only outlet when we moved to this country ... He always took me to gay bars and I loved it. I always encountered sensitive people who looked much nicer, and seemed to enjoy themselves more. They seemed freer. I suppose because of that I became gay myself in a sense. I became like a gay man.
                    GRACE JONES

I was really discovered by gay audiences. They are very knowledgeable about music.
                    MAUREEN McGOVERN

Let me say, a more artistic, appreciative group of people for the arts does not exist ... They are more knowledgeable, more loving of the arts. They make the average male look stupid.
                    BETTE DAVIS

Sophia Loren: "God made homosexuals, so He must love them. I love them, too."

To see that the gay following is still with me, it makes me feel I'm still happening, because for some reason, it's not easy to please a gay following. I mean, they're very, very bright . . . There's something about the gay following, that if you're not "in," then I have to go and do a little research and homework to get back on the track . . . Entertainers who consider themselves professionals and don't want or appreciate gay fans, I feel, are really stupid.

PATTI LA BELLE

———

Every star, female star, must have this following. I don't know why homosexuals like me. Maybe, just because I like them. God made homosexuals, so He must love them. I love them, too.

SOPHIA LOREN

. . . now I've become a champion of the homosexual cause . . . and it's because I sit in group therapy and watch tortured intellectuals who've struggled all their lives with their homosexuality. When I hear the things that come out of these people and when I see what pious clergymen and fearful heterosexuals impose on them, I *do* want to speak out on their behalf.

BLAKE EDWARDS

I'm a supporter of gay rights. And not a closet supporter either. From the time I was a kid, I have never been able to understand attacks upon the gay community. There are so many qualities that make up a human being . . . by the time I get through with all the things that I really admire about people, what they do with their private parts is probably so low on the list that it is irrelevant.

PAUL NEWMAN

People who can't think of anything else but whether the person you love is indented or convex should be doomed not to think of anything else but that, and so miss the other ninety-five percent of life.

ROBERT TOWNE, writer and director of the 1982 film Personal Best

---

About a year ago I was a guest on a network news show in New York. They were showing film clips from a gay pride parade down Fifth Avenue, but they only decided to show the part with men in dresses and heels. I had seen the parade, and there were men in business suits as well. After showing the film, the newsperson made some comments, and I found the comments extremely offensive. "This is what's wrong with the media," I said. "You show a fringe position. You show one point of view. You're closing the minds of the people by not showing them what the reality is." I got up and walked out, and I've never been asked back again.

Actress KATHLEEN NOLAN, former president of the Screen Actors Guild and best known for her role as Kate on the TV *series* The Real McCoys

John Wayne: You won't see him jumping for joy over homosexuality.

I can really understand the suffering of the gay community because, in certain ways, I've had the same problems myself. I am *sympatica* because I've had to go through discrimination. I've been exploited and I know how it feels: having to be made into something you're not.

Fifties sex symbol MAMIE VAN DOREN

———

So I see no reason to jump with joy because somebody is a gay and I don't see any reason for waving a flag for all the wonderful things gays have done for the world . . . any more than you'd say, "Oh boy, hooray for the tuberculosis victim!" It's abnormal to me. Now as far as having them live their own life, I feel that a man has a right to live his life the way he wishes — as long as he doesn't interfere with me having my rights. So I have nothing against them, but I certainly see no reason to jump with joy about it.

JOHN WAYNE (1907-1979)

Real men are a dying breed in this country. There aren't any John Waynes anymore — in show business or on the outside; it's all over; all you've got now walking around is a bunch of sissies.
MIKE CONNORS

———

I remember when I did *Lust for Life* and we had a showing of it, afterwards at a party I had a talk with John Wayne and he was rather upset. He said, "Kirk, what the hell are you doing, a guy like you, you shouldn't be playing parts like that." He was upset that I should play this character [painter Vincent Van Gogh] who had a homosexual problem with Gauguin. He said, "What are you trying to do?" *KIRK DOUGLAS*

———

I remember one of the lawyers saying when he read the script that he would like to wash his hands, that there was nothing he could do to stop us, but he would like to wash his hands and clean out his mouth . . . That's how it was in those days.
English actor DIRK BOGARDE, on initial reaction to the script of the 1961 film Victim, *in which Bogarde portrayed a homosexual lawyer*

———

I was surprised how shocked they were. One said, "But your magnificent voice. What can you do with it to make it homosexual?" Are they unaware that some of the greatest voices in the theater belong to homosexuals? I hardly knew how to answer when they asked, over and over, how I could play such a horrid part . . . the reactions of these people worry me, for they are supposed to be somewhat sophisticated, more so than their readers.
RICHARD BURTON, on the hostile reaction of some members of the press to his and Rex Harrison's roles as gay lovers in the 1969 film Staircase

———

. . .we're too old, too famous, and too rich to worry about the consequences.
REX HARRISON, asked if he thought his

and Richard Burton's careers would be hurt by their roles in Staircase

———

Hollywood is like something from the dark ages. There is no town more homophobic than Hollywood at every level of the industry. You go on the sets, they're rednecked. I see actors who I know are gay, who I've seen in a gay bar the night before, who act like they don't know another gay person. They wear wedding bands. It's that devastating here. The gay casting people are the most homophobic of all. They are closeted and they're terrified for their jobs.

Openly gay actor MICHAEL KEARNS

———

I myself was once badly burned when I cast a gay friend in a movie without even realizing that he had some effeminate mannerisms. That movie had the only Mafia hit man in television history who lisped.

An anonymous gay television producer, quoted in TV Guide

———

Homosexuality is a way of life that I've grown accustomed to. I have the same feelings as anyone else. It just happens that I like my career so much that I'd like people to remember my music and not my personality ... What's the big deal about my sexuality? Anything as controversial as homosexuality is boring!

Singer JOHNNY MATHIS

———

Look, I know lots of gays in Hollywood, and most of them are nice guys. Some have tried it on with me, but I've said, "Come on, now. You've got the wrong guy."

ROCK HUDSON (1925-1985), asked in a 1980 interview if he was homosexual

———

I wish more prominent people could bring themselves to come out of their closets. Nearly always the world knows who they are already, however hard they try to fool it. Coming out would actually make their lives less isolated and troubled; it would give them

Johnny Mathis: His fans couldn't have cared less.

faith and courage in themselves. And isn't that worth far more than the notoriety they already enjoy?

CHRISTOPHER ISHERWOOD

———

I don't think most actors want to come out of the closet. I have a personal theory that it's not because they think it's going to hurt their career; I think it's because they really are ashamed of who they are. Nine times out of ten, if a person is a well-loved figure, or a good actor, they can get away with it. Let's see, who could you be and not get away with it? Someone who had absolutely no talent and only looks ... Tom Selleck. Tom Selleck's career would be ruined because his career is based on his heterosexuality.

Writer and critic VITO RUSSO,
author of The Celluloid Closet

———

No romantic leading man will ever work, in my opinion, if he says he's gay. You don't see any of them doing it, do you?

Syndicated gossip columnist LIZ SMITH

Michael Caine: He told one gay magazine, "Most big stars would never play a homosexual role, fearing what their fans might think. I'm not that type of actor."

It's up to the performer ... If he's not going to enjoy a continuance of his career, if it's a clear case that his career will be threatened — I'd suggest staying in the closet, professionally, you understand.

Actor ED ASNER, former president of the
Screen Actors Guild

The gay business really hurt me. A lot of radio stations stopped playing my records.

ELTON JOHN, who acknowledged his
bisexuality to the press in 1976

People sometimes think I'm gay because I once played a gay in a movie. It's funny. Audiences don't think you're a murderer if you play a murderer, but they do think you're gay if you play a gay.

Actor PERRY KING

If you play a gay role, it sticks more than it does if an actor were to play a murderer or a psychopath. There were a couple of producers that I heard through friends were convinced that I was gay and that if I was going out with a woman it was a front.
HARRY HAMLIN, who played a gay novelist in the 1982 film Making Love

Look, an actor only plays one gay in his career if he has any sense. If he does more than that he ends up being another Franklin Pangborn. I will never play another homosexual.
GENE BARRY, one of the stars of the musical La Cage aux Folles

I've done it all. I've been a gay, a killer, a lunatic, an adulterer, a seducer. A good time was had by all.
MICHAEL CAINE

I want to play homosexuals and lovers and gamblers and thieves.
Actor CHARLIE SHEEN, on his desire not to be typecast as "an all-American boy"

I didn't think I would enjoy *The Love Machine*, but I ended up absolutely loving it. It's an extraordinary film. I play a screaming faggot from beginning to end. An absolutely bitchy, overt, pushy, *snarling* fag . . . It was very funny. There's a fight scene where Dyan Cannon finally bashes me over the head with an Oscar.
British actor DAVID HEMMINGS

We've become the Laurel and Hardy of homosexuality.
French actor MICHEL SERRAULT, on his and Ugo Tognazzi's roles in the La Cage aux Folles *films*

I asked my agent, "Would you play a homosexual if your father

were running for office?" He said, "Sure." But if I were *really* gay, I
couldn't, I wouldn't, do it.

> Actor *JOHN DUKAKIS, son of
> Massachusetts Governor and presidential
> aspirant Michael Dukakis, on his role as one of
> Harry Hamlin's gay "tricks" in* Making Love

———

They told me they'd called a lot of gay actors, but nobody wanted
to do Emory. I guess a real homosexual might be too inhibited
... I didn't do anything special to prepare for it, although the
walk took a lot of practice. But I already knew how to lisp because
I'd been telling gay jokes since I was a kid.

> Actor *CLIFF GORMAN, on his role as the
> effeminate gay man Emory in the stage and
> screen versions of* The Boys in the Band, *in
> a 1968* New York Times *interview entitled
> "You Don't Have to Be One to Play One."
> During the interview, Gorman conspicuously
> drank two beers (the beer is mentioned three
> times in the interview), played country-western
> music ("the only kind of music that really moves
> him"), and wore a "John Wayne style" bandana
> around his neck; Gorman's "incredibly beautiful"
> wife was also much in evidence. Later in the
> interview, Gorman characterized the part of
> Emory as "a loser"; not to be outdone,* Times
> *reporter Judy Klemesrud described Emory as a
> "pansy ... the show's only swishy, 42nd Street
> stereotype fag — the pathetic kind that most
> people associate with homosexuality."*

———

Yes, I'm gay, when I'm on that stage. If the role required me to
suck off Horst, I'd do it.

> *RICHARD GERE, on his role as Max, a
> homosexual incarcerated in a Nazi concentration
> camp, in Martin Sherman's Broadway play,*
> Bent. *In one scene, Gere's character verbally
> makes love to another inmate, Horst, while the
> two of them are standing three feet apart. Gere*

Richard Gere: "If the role required me to suck off Horst, I'd do it."

Michael Ontkean and Harry Hamlin in the 1982 film *Making Love.*

said of the role, "I suppose some people thought it was daring, but it wasn't — the stage is different, everybody knows you leave the character at the stage door."

I just closed my eyes and thought of England.

Actor PETER FINCH (1916-1977), asked how he prepared for his on-screen kiss with actor Murray Head in John Schlesinger's 1971 film Sunday, Bloody Sunday

...like in *Making Love,* those two actors Ontkean and Hamlin were granting interviews about how difficult it was to kiss another man, about how they had to think of their girlfriends while they were doing it. What a load of crap! Homosexual actors have been kissing women in films for fifty years without saying that it turned their stomach, you know.

ARMISTEAD MAUPIN

[Director Arthur] Hiller went pretty far, further than I thought he'd go. They undress each other and kiss. They make love. Of course, there's enough footage so that if we have to pull something out we can. I mean, if they run screaming from the theater in Omaha.

BARRY SANDLER, who wrote the screenplay
for Making Love, *on the film's explicit*
homosexual love scenes

I don't think audiences are going to hit the screen with their canes. I think we're past that.

Director JAMES IVORY, on the homosexual
love scenes in his 1987 screen adaptation of
E.M. Forster's Maurice

I'm a prude as well as a snob. When Pat and I went to see *Sister George* we stared at the floor a lot of the time. It was embarrassing to see something like that sitting with a crowd of people in a movie house.

RAQUEL WELCH, on going with her hus-
band to see the 1968 film The Killing of
Sister George, *based on Frank Marcus's play*
about lesbianism; ironically, Welch made the
remarks during a publicity interview for her own
X-rated film, Myra Breckenridge.

With my mother there, I thought I was going to have a heart attack.

MARIEL HEMINGWAY, who sat behind

Johnny Weissmuller, and the thighs that drove Cheetah to ecstasy.

her parents during a screening of Personal
Best, *in which Hemingway had several lesbian
love scenes*

In his movie *Risky Business* the scene with [Tom Cruise] dancing
with just his underwear on has to be the most erotic in movie his-

tory. I took my mother to see that movie and I swear when that scene appeared on the screen I creamed in my pants. When the movie was over and it was time to leave, I was so embarrassed because of my wet and sticky situation. But when I saw my mother leaving with her dripping panties, I knew she had the same reaction that I had.

> *Reader letter to* In Touch *magazine,*
> *January 1984*

———

Out where they say,
Let us be gay!
I'm going Hollywood!

> *BING CROSBY, in the 1933 movie musical*
> Going Hollywood

———

Damn queers. They're taking over Hollywood.

> *Former television exercise instructor JACK*
> *LaLANNE, in a 1979 interview*

———

Cheetah, that bastard, bit me whenever he could. The apes were all homosexuals, eager to wrap their paws around John's thighs. They were jealous of me, and I loathed them.

> *Actress MAUREEN O'SULLIVAN, on her*
> *role as Jane, opposite Johnny Weissmuller and*
> *Cheetah the chimp, in some of the early Tarzan*
> *movies, from 1932 to 1942*

———

. . . if you removed all of the homosexuals and homosexual influence from what is generally regarded as American culture, you would be pretty much left with *Let's Make a Deal.*

> *FRAN LEBOWITZ*

———

. . let's face it, sweetheart — without Jews, fags and gypsies, there *is* no theater.

> *MEL BROOKS, in the 1983 film* To Be Or
> Not to Be

WORD OF MOUTH

I have all the normal, violent repugnance to homosexuality — if it is really normal, which nowadays one is sometimes provoked to doubt.

GEORGE BERNARD SHAW (1856-1950)

There was one point where our daughters, Gloria and Barbara, told me that they didn't want to hold hands with their little girl-friends anymore. They were afraid people would think they were homosexuals.

ANITA BRYANT

If adjustment is necessary, it should be made primarily with regard to the position the homosexual occupies in present-day society, and society should more often be treated than the homosexual.

Psychotherapist DR. HARRY BENJAMIN

Love and loyalty to an individual can run counter to the claims of the State. When they do — down with the State, say I, which means that the State would down me.

E.M. FORSTER (1879-1970)

...perhaps this love, which according to some people is out-rageous, escapes the changing seasons and the wanings of love by

Samuel M. Steward: With
his dog.

being controlled with invisible severity, nourished on very little,
permitted to live gropingly and without a goal, its unique flower
being a mutual trust such as that other love can never plumb or
comprehend . . . So great is such a love that by its grace, a half century can pass by like a day of exquisite and delicious retirement.

> *COLETTE (1873-1954)*

It would be nice I suppose to have a man around the house but if
not, you settle for a dog.

> *Writer SAMUEL STEWARD*
> *(also known as "Phil Andros")*

They have found a substance in marijuana which is very close to
the female hormone. Some men find they are developing feminine
characteristics.

> *RONALD REAGAN, during his 1976*
> *campaign for the Republican presidential*
> *nomination*

All my life I wanted to look like Liz Taylor. Now I find that Liz Taylor is beginning to look like me.

DIVINE (1945-1988), in 1981

. . . there was something about Divine that both intrigued me and amused me. For one thing, I thought he was very talented. When we were filming in Santa Fe, I only saw him as a man for about one hour out of each day. After that, it was like he was my girlfriend. In fact, I almost forgot he was a man until he said, "Listen, honey, underneath this skirt beats a rod of steel. . ."

LANIE KAZAN, who co-starred with Divine and Tab Hunter in the 1985 film Lust in the Dust

---

The great bulk of the gay population . . . goes to work in the morning and comes home at night, like anybody else. It runs the gamut as far as ideology is concerned, and I suspect that, in the majority, it is probably conservative.

Former San Francisco Mayor
DIANNE FEINSTEIN

Homosexuals are disco babies and Goldwater Republicans.

ROBERT L. LIVINGSTON,
gay member of the New York City Commission on Human Rights, in 1979

I get tired of hearing the pissing and moaning about clones. Because people who choose to wear clone costumes are choosing to be publicly homosexual. I think that's a political act itself. I would endorse them over any coat-and-tie faggot any day of the week.

ARMISTEAD MAUPIN

If I went onstage in a business suit, they would think I was crazy. It's like putting Marlene Dietrich in a housedress.

LIBERACE (1919-1987)

Divine and Lanie Kazan in the 1985 film *Lust in the Dust.*

I'm a drag addict. Not a drug addict.

> *BOY GEORGE, in a 1986 interview with the*
> London Daily Mail

———

That's all England needs: another queen who can't dress.

> *JOAN RIVERS, on Boy George*

———

To me, the drag queen is one of the main heroes (or heroines) of the gay world. The courage required for her merely to step out on the street in drag is perhaps a thousand times more than the courage that is required for any of the rest of us. She's almost a sacrificial figure, absorbing all the hatred that is leveled on us from other quarters.

> *Writer JOHN RECHY*

———

I have gotten millions of letters from drag queens. One I'll never forget wrote and said, "I hear you're making a movie about poor white trash that turns into rich white trash. I'll tell you what I'd do if I was rich white trash. I'd get myself three maids and just sit in a wheelchair, so I'd never have to walk, and take quaaludes the rest of my life."

> *JOHN WATERS, director of*
> Pink Flamingos *and* Hairspray

———

It's a good thing that I was born a woman, or I'd have been a drag queen.

> *DOLLY PARTON*

———

There are many aspects of the contemporary gay subculture that I find ridiculous, but nothing could be more ridiculous than to say, as some critics have, that I am anti-homosexual simply because I do not embrace every twitty gay fad that comes along. I think that a lifetime of listening to disco music is a high price to pay for one's sexual preference.

> *QUENTIN CRISP*

Dolly Parton: There, but for the grace of God, goes she...

They talk about "gay sensibility"; I've never seen any sign of it. I've never seen any sign of "heterosexual sensibility." I always use the example of what did Lyndon Johnson have in common with Bertrand Russell, except that they both liked to fuck women . . . Did they share a heterosexual sensibility? I think not.

GORE VIDAL

I don't think there is a "gay lifestyle." I think that's superficial crap, all that talk about gay culture. A couple of restaurants on Castro Street and a couple of magazines do not constitute culture. Michelangelo is culture. Virginia Woolf is culture. So let's don't confuse our terms. Wearing earrings is not culture. . .

Writer RITA MAE BROWN

Oh Mary, it takes a fairy to make something pretty.

Emory, in MART CROWLEY's play
The Boys in the Band, *1968*

In the artistic society of London one man in three is homosexual, which is very bad on the ladies, but not at all bad on me.

Mystery writer RAYMOND CHANDLER
(1888-1959)

I should like to know why nearly every man that approaches greatness tends to homosexuality, whether he admits it or not. . .

D.H. LAWRENCE (1885-1930)

Take your average straight lawyer from Des Moines, who's married with three kids — his taste is terrible. Take a gay lawyer in the same city, and he'll look a lot better.

Designer EGON VON FURSTENBERG

Whoever designed the Nazi uniforms had to be gay. Those were the sexiest men I have ever seen in my life, and it was mostly because of their uniforms — the high boots and the close-cut jackets.

TOM OF FINLAND

I want the Lacoste people to do a robe for me. Don't they owe it to us? With just a little alligator...

Superior Court Judge STEPHEN M.
LACHS, the country's first openly gay judge,
appointed in 1979 by California Governor
Jerry Brown

We're not waving any banners. If I'm interviewed now, it's as a musician. If I want to be gay after tea time, it's entirely my affair.

HOLLY JOHNSON, lead vocalist of "Frankie
Goes to Hollywood"

This business of "show me a happy homosexual and I'll show you a gay corpse" isn't the way it really is. That's the exception, not the rule. Lots of people manage to solve their emotional hang-ups; they make the adjustments that have to be made.

JOHN SCHLESINGER

I thought he would be a wonderful husband. He was charming, his career was red hot, he was gorgeous, 6'6" tall. How many women would have said no? If I had heard things about his being homosexual, I just put them in the back of my mind. So what if it was true? We were having an affair, and he asked me to marry him.

PHYLLIS GATES, Rock Hudson's ex-wife;
Hudson and Gates were married in 1955,
divorced in 1958

I have to have a boy. For a year I've been faithful; I haven't had a boy and I'm going crazy. Can you fix me up?

ROCK HUDSON, to friend Mark Miller,
after Hudson had been married for a year

Rock Hudson: "I have found out I have AIDS."

Hi, this note shall remain anonymous for obvious reasons. Since we have had intimate sexual contact where sperm has passed between us, I feel it is only fair to tell you that I have found out I have AIDS. I am sorry to tell you this. I suggest you have tests made to make sure you're okay.

> *ROCK HUDSON, in a note sent to his former boyfriends, after he was diagnosed with AIDS in 1984*

A poor, beloved American is lying dying in a hospital and all our media can worry about is whether Linda Evans is going to get the disease.

> *Writer LARRY KRAMER, shortly after public disclosures that Rock Hudson had AIDS*

I don't like jokes about AIDS. That ticks me off. Anybody telling jokes about Rock Hudson should be slapped on the wrist — or have his face ripped off, depending on the tastelessness of the joke.

> *Former football star turned actor*
> *JOHN MATUSZAK*

I do try to combat what I see as a prevailing American prejudice, an attitude which is against sex — as if sex can be ignored or dispensed with. I think that American anti-sexualism is the context for what's happening today. I think that a lot of gay people have reverted to the traditional American anti-sexual attitudes, saying, "We can do without it." And then of course telling others that they can do without it too.

> *Playwright ROBERT CHESLEY*

I have a husband, and we have a dog, and we live in the country. It's what I always wanted.

> *Gay comedian TERRY SWEENEY*

I fell in love with Terry the minute I saw his impersonation of Angie Dickinson in her shooting position from *Police Woman*.

> *Comedy writer LANIER LANEY,*
> *Terry Sweeney's lover*

An extremely attractive girl came down to our training center in Mexico. She was a lesbian and she was very active sexually, but all of her energy was devoted to making it with girls. She was at an LSD session at one of our cottages and went down to the beach and saw this young man in a bathing suit and — flash! . . . Her subsequent sexual choices were almost exclusively members of the opposite sex.

> *Former drug guru TIMOTHY LEARY, on the*
> *ability of LSD to "cure" homosexuality*

Certainly not. For while it is always tempting to opt for any kind of uniformity which would automatically reduce human conflict, only a fool would reach into some giant computer that nobody understands and start yanking out transistors.

Researcher C.A. TRIPP, author of The Homosexual Matrix, *after being asked whether, given the power to do so, he would eliminate homosexuality from future generations of humanity*

PRIDE AND PREJUDICE

Now, listen, you queer. Stop calling me a crypto-Nazi or I'll sock you in your goddamn face and you'll stay plastered.

> *Conservative columnist WILLIAM F. BUCKLEY, to Gore Vidal, during a live telecast from the 1968 Democratic Convention in Chicago; Buckley made the remarks after Vidal referred to him as a "crypto-Nazi."*

———

What do you know about men, you fat, ugly faggot?!

> *Actor HENRY FONDA (1905-1982), to Charles Laughton, during rehearsals of the Broadway play* The Caine Mutiny Court Martial, *in the early 1950s; Fonda was furious at Laughton, who was directing the play, for cutting some of his scenes and for hiring handsome young extras whose looks might have upstaged Fonda; producer Paul Gregory later wrote that Fonda's treatment of Laughton "was absolutely the cruelest thing I've ever seen."*

———

This deadly, winking, sniggering, snuggling, scent-impregnated, chromium-plated, luminous, quivering, giggling, fruit-flavored, mincing, ice-covered heap of mother-love...

> London Daily Mirror *columnist WILLIAM CONNOR, in a 1956 attack on entertainer*

Henry Fonda: As with many people, prejudice lay just beneath the surface.

Liberace; Connor's remarks prompted Liberace to sue both the columnist and the newspaper for libel for implying he was homosexual; Liberace won the suit, but almost thirty years later, after Liberace died of AIDS and it was revealed that he had in fact been homosexual, the Daily Mirror *asked the entertainer's estate for its money back.*

I'll bet *the army* burned *his* draft card.

Comic DICK MARTIN, after the premiere of falsetto singer Tiny Tim on "Rowan and Martin's Laugh-In" in 1968

The cop-out, immoral lifestyle of the tragic misfits espoused by your publication has no place in organized athletics at any level. Your colossal gall in attempting to extend your perversion to an area of total manhood is just simply unthinkable.

TOM MEE, public relations director for the Minnesota Twins baseball team, in response to a 1975 query by The Advocate *about gays in athletics*

When someone says, "I'm from Ferrysburg," it causes chuckles. Some people even refer to the mayor and council as the leading fairies. It does become an irritant.

LEON STILLE, mayor of Ferrysburg, Michigan, after ongoing jokes about the town's name prompted some angry residents to crusade for the name to be changed; the head of a gay rights group in nearby Ann Arbor told the press, "For folks to take this as a civic issue reflects the deep prejudice in this society."

Some aspects of prejudice and discrimination can never be reached by laws. I wish that my poor power of expression permitted me to convey to those who are not gay the depth of despair and suffering society inflicts in a thousand subtle and not so subtle ways on the homosexual ... What gays experience is a rejection not of their actions but of who they are constitutionally, a rejection of their very nature and being ... The really lucky ones are able to deal with this eventually and go on with life, though few are ever reconciled fully to this cruel treatment.

Former Congressman ROBERT BAUMAN,
in an address to the American Bar Association in
1983

When you're gay, you always feel separate. It's like guard dogs are pacing back and forth keeping something in you protected and private.

TERRY SWEENEY

It is a great shock at the age of five or six to find that in a world of Gary Coopers you are the Indian.

JAMES BALDWIN (1924-1988)

I feel that the greatest prejudice in the world is against the homosexual. I'm Jewish, I grew up in the Midwest where there were a lot of prejudices but nothing like the violent prejudice that cuts across all racial groups, at various times, against homosexuals.

DR. DAVID GOTTLIEB,
author of The Gay Tapes

Americans have a very low tolerance for differentness, whether it's racial, ethnic, or sexual. Despite our rhetoric about individualism, we are a desperately conforming people.

MARTIN DUBERMAN

We all know a fag is a homosexual gentleman who has just left the room.

TRUMAN CAPOTE

It's like a sort of vanity to say that we're hated. I don't think the average working-class person hates gay people. I think they're scared of them, they don't understand them, but I don't think there's any malice on the part of the majority.

Gay activist JERRY SILVERMAN

———

...what irritates me is the bland way people go around saying, "Oh, our attitude has changed. We don't dislike these people any more." But by the strangest coincidence, they haven't taken away the injustice; the laws are still on the books.

CHRISTOPHER ISHERWOOD

———

Because there has been a tremendous increase in societal acceptance of gay people, those without historical perspective imagine this acceptance to be permanent and likely to increase with time. Unfortunately, cultural tolerance is like an ocean tide. It can reach a high watermark and then recede out of sight.

Writer DONALD VINING

———

It is easy to stand up for the right of a black as a human being, but hard to side with a "queer." No matter how closely the white civil rights enthusiast tries to identify with the plight of the Negro, blackness can never rub off on him. The aura of "immorality" can.

Attorney WALTER BARNETT, author of
Sexual Freedom and the Constitution

———

What we have to acknowledge is that our own passivity has given the opposition a free rein to be the loudest voices ... We are the last acceptable prejudice, and we've got to say that intolerance is intolerable.

VIRGINIA APUZZO, former director of the
National Gay Task Force

———

The greatest obstacle that gay people have is their fear of rejection on account of homosexuality.

Gay San Francisco City Supervisor
HARRY BRITT

Virginia Apuzzo: We need to fight our own passivity.

One of the interesting things about the homosexual minority is that it is really the only minority that has a choice of "coming out." If you're black, you're black. You can't evade that.

Writer MERLE MILLER (1919-1986)

I wish that homosexuals were born with a little horn in the middle of their forehead so we couldn't hide so easily. At least if you can't hide, you have to stand up and fight.

HARVEY FIERSTEIN

I'm not from the school which says "We mustn't fight back and be just like they are." I'd *like* to kill somebody. I really would.

Writer DANIEL CURZON

For Christ's sake, open your mouths; don't you people get tired of being stepped on?

BETTE MIDLER, in an interview with
Leo Skir for Gay *magazine*

The folkways of our culture are filled with images of homosexuals as sick, evil, less than human . . . At the same time, the law itself epitomizes this attitude. The very fact that our laws make homosexuality a crime puts the stamp of approval on the idea that "queers" are animals . . . The society's values make the homosexual a "faggot," easy prey. . .

> *DR. JOHN MONEY, professor of medical psychology at Johns Hopkins University*

You must realize there are thousands upon thousands of frustrated *angry* people waiting to unleash a fury that can and will eradicate the malignancies which blight our beautiful city . . . I am not going to be forced out of San Francisco by splinter groups of radicals, social deviates, incorrigibles. . .

> *From a campaign brochure for DAN WHITE (1946-1985), the former San Francisco policeman who successfully ran for a position on the city's Board of Supervisors and who later murdered Mayor George Moscone and gay city supervisor Harvey Milk; White committed suicide shortly after his release from prison*

If I were the chief of police, I would get me a hundred good men, give them each a baseball bat, and have them walk down Duval Street and dare one of these freaks to stick his head over the sidewalk. That is the way it was done in Key West in the days I remember and love.

> *Baptist minister MORRIS WRIGHT of Key West, Florida; Wright's remarks appeared in an ad he took out in a Key West newspaper in January 1979; many of Key West's gay establishments are located on Duval Street.*

Maybe they weren't punks at all, but New York drama critics. That mugging received better and more extensive publicity than anything I ever wrote.

> *TENNESSEE WILLIAMS, after he and a friend were attacked by a gang of youths outside*

*a gay bar in Key West, Florida in 1979; on
another occasion, a group of teenagers stood
outside Williams' Key West home and threw beer
cans and firecrackers, while chanting, "Come on
out, faggot!"*

———

I regard it as a tragedy that people of a differing sexual orientation
find themselves proscribed in a world that has so little understanding for homosexuals and that displays such gross indifference for
sexual gradations and variations and the great significance they
have for living. It is completely foreign to me to wish to regard such
people as less valuable, less moral, incapable of noble sentiments
and behavior.

*Social activist EMMA GOLDMAN
(1869-1940)*

———

I can't understand any discussion of gays and lesbians as if they
were something immoral or unsatisfactory — they're doing just
what nature wants them to do.

*Architect and writer BUCKMINSTER
FULLER (1895-1983)*

———

Homosexuality is assuredly no advantage, but it is nothing to be
ashamed of, no vice, no degradation, it cannot be classified as an
illness . . . It is a great injustice to persecute homosexuality as a
crime, and cruelty too.

*SIGMUND FREUD (1856-1939), in a
1935 letter to the mother of a homosexual*

———

Homosexuality is a sickness, just as are baby-rape or wanting to
become head of General Motors.

ELDRIDGE CLEAVER,
Soul On Ice, *1968*

———

I fought for the civil rights of homosexuals twenty years ago and
argued that they should be regarded as full and equal citizens.

However, I do not believe homosexuality is "just another life style." I believe these people suffer from a severe personality disorder. Granted some are sicker than others, but sick they are and all the fancy rhetoric of the American Psychiatric Association will not change it.

> *ANN LANDERS, in 1976, after the American Psychiatric Association dropped homosexuality from its list of mental illnesses*

I am reminded of a colleague who reiterated "all my homosexual patients are quite sick" — to which I finally replied "so are all my heterosexual patients."

> *Psychoanalyst ERNEST VAN DEN HAAG*

You're neither unnatural, nor abominable, nor mad; you're as much a part of what people call nature as anyone else; only you're unexplained as yet — you've not got your niche in creation.

> *RADCLYFFE HALL,*
> The Well of Loneliness, *1928*

We have forced gay people into the red-light districts, forced them to meet each other in bars and lurid places — then we call them promiscuous sinners.

> *ADELE STARR, founding president of Parents and Friends of Lesbians and Gays*

Let us, once and for all, get rid of the word "gay" as a euphemism for homosexual. Gay means "merry, cheerful and lighthearted." The homos I have seen are a depressing eyesore on the landscape of humanity. They are neither merry nor cheerful ... A better word for homosexual is "queer," because that is what they are.

> *Reader letter to Ann Landers in 1980; Landers replied, in part, "I agree that large numbers of homosexuals are neither merry nor cheerful, but they can call themselves anything they want as far as I am concerned."*

Regarding the use of "gay" . . . They aren't gay to me and a lot of other people; they are homosexuals and should be so identified at all times, unless "gay" is in the title of the organization, or is used in a quote.

1978 staff memorandum from former Wall Street Journal *editor FRED TAYLOR, after the term "gay people" inadvertently appeared in a* Journal *headline*

"Gay" used to be one of the most agreeable words in the language. Its appropriation by a notably morose group is an act of piracy.

Historian and John F. Kennedy speechwriter ARTHUR SCHLESINGER JR.

I'd also purge the queers. I despise them worst of all. They're one of the ugliest problems of our society, and they must be removed — I don't know if with gas, or what, just so they don't poison society . . . They're the ultimate symbol of a decaying civilization.

American Nazi Party leader GEORGE LINCOLN ROCKWELL (1918-1967), in a 1966 interview

Are homosexuals social outcasts? My God. Christopher Isherwood, Howard Brown, Merle Miller, Sidney Abbott, John Maynard Keynes. Are these people social outcasts? Some of the most moral men I know are homosexuals.

Psychologist DR. EVELYN HOOKER, author of several pioneering studies on homosexuality in the 1950s

I am here tonight to express my solidarity with the gay and lesbian community in your struggle for civil and human rights in America and around the world. I believe all Americans who believe in freedom, tolerance and human rights have a responsibility to oppose bigotry and prejudice based on sexual orientation.

CORETTA SCOTT KING, widow of

*Martin Luther King Jr., at a 1986 gay rights
fundraiser*

———

Now we had all this mob over the weekend, which itself was a
disheartening spectacle . . . We have to call a spade a spade and a
perverted human being a perverted human being. . .

> *U.S. Senator JESSE HELMS (R-North
> Carolina), on the gay rights march on
> Washington D.C. in October 1987*

———

Gay Rights parades that followed in Stonewall's wake were to be
enjoyed as spicy local color on televisions news shows — as Ziggy
Stardust revues with placards, perfect for leading into the weather
— rather than as harbingers of a political movement gathering
critical mass.

> *Writer FRANK RICH*

———

Parades in New York are usually masquerades . . . But the point of
the Gay Pride parade has always been different; not that these people marching are, above all, homosexuals, but that these homosexuals marching are, above all, people. . .

> *From an editorial in* THE NEW YORKER,
> *on the 1987 Gay Pride march in New York
> City*

———

The gay movement will be successful when a young woman or
man can acknowledge his or her homosexuality to family, friends,
and co-workers without any sense of shame and without feeling in
any way second class. When this can happen, Gay Pride marches
will indeed be redundant; there will be no reason to proclaim our
pride in being gay if it is recognized as a perfectly ordinary and
acceptable way of living one's emotional and sexual life.

> *Writer DENNIS ALTMAN*

———

They go about saying they're just like ordinary people — which is never going to work because ordinary people never go around saying they're ordinary.

QUENTIN CRISP

In the gay rights movement, we try to emphasize that we are the same as everybody else except for what we do in bed. The American Indian cultures I studied do just the opposite; they emphasize the difference, but instead of seeing that difference as abnormal, deviant, or threatening, they see it as a "specialness," an extra gift.

WALTER WILLIAMS, author of The Spirit and the Flesh: Sexual Diversity in American Indian Culture, *1987*

. . . we're constantly having conservative homosexuals say that we need to get married, to adopt children, join the army . . . In effect the heterosexual is turned into a parent and we're saying we're nice children, and we're going to be just like you. I think it's very special to be homosexual and I don't want that kind of heterosexual shit put on me. . .

JOHN RECHY

Imitating straight lifestyles doesn't work for homosexuals.

ARTHUR BELL

Affirming the good in gay had a deep emotional and political value for us, but intellectually and historically, I think "Gay is good" is terribly superficial. It trivializes us; it's banal.

Historian and writer JONATHAN KATZ

Black Pride and Gay Pride are dangerous slogans like White Pride or Straight Pride. Gay and Black are not achievements but accidents of birth. One must not be ashamed, but that's not the same as being proud. Pride should lie only in what one does with one's Blackness or Gayness.

NED ROREM

Homosexual men and women are best understood when they are seen as whole human beings, not just in terms of what they do sexually. And that, surely, is the important point about any class of human beings that are in any way indistinguishable from others. By virtue of the fact that a person is a human being, whatever his or her biological or behavioral traits (so long as they are in no way damaging to others), the person has a full right to his or her growth and development as a human being.

Anthropologist ASHLEY MONTAGU

———

Do you think homosexuals are revolting? You bet your sweet ass we are!

From a 1969 leaflet inviting people to the founding meeting of the Gay Liberation Front in New York City

AIDS

Some Reagan Administration supporters have gone on record as saying that AIDS is God's judgment on homosexuals, but you have never heard one of them say that Legionnaire's Disease was God's judgment on the right-wing views of the American Legion.

H. CARL McCALL, chairman of the New York State Division of Human Rights

The poor homosexuals — they have declared war upon nature, and now nature is exacting an awful retribution.

Conservative commentator and former Reagan aide PATRICK BUCHANAN, writing about AIDS

What we're seeing here is the re-diseasing of homosexuality.

RICK CRANE, program director of AIDS/Kaposi's Sarcoma Research and Education Foundation in San Francisco

It's a fascinating problem. We get excited about it until we remember it is killing people.

DR. ROBERT BIGGAR, of the National Cancer Institute, on the challenges of AIDS research

The panic is here. I know lots of people who worry about every bruise they get, who worry about a swollen lymph node, the night sweats, even a slight fever. Every gay man I know worries about AIDS — I mean, *profoundly* worries.

PAT GOURLEY, *of the Gay and Lesbian*
Community Center of Colorado

...the psychological impact of AIDS on the gay community is tremendous. It has done more to undermine the feelings of self-esteem than anything Anita Bryant could have ever done. Some people are saying, "Maybe we *are* wrong — maybe this is a punishment."

New York City judge RICHARD FAILLA

Come on, it's a virus of some sort — it's just a disease ... God doesn't send you to the basement if you're bad.

TED McCLOUD, a man with AIDS,
quoted in Newsweek

If we accept the notion of Jerry Falwell and others that AIDS represents God's punishment to erring homosexuals, then it stands to reason that lesbians — virtually untouched by AIDS or sexually transmitted diseases — must be God's chosen people.

Letter to the Editor, Newsweek

It is not easy to know the intentions of God himself.

POPE JOHN PAUL II, asked, during his
1987 trip to the U.S., whether AIDS was
God's punishment against homosexuals

There's a moral laxity around. Herpes and AIDS have come as the great plagues to teach us all a lesson. It was fine to have sexual freedom, but it was abused. Apparently, the original AIDS sufferers were having 500 or 600 contacts a year, and they are now inflicting it on heterosexuals. That's bloody scary. It's like the

Joan Collins: Upholding the nation's morals.

Roman Empire. Wasn't everybody running around just covered with syphilis? And then it was destroyed by the volcano.

> *JOAN COLLINS, in a 1984 interview in* Playboy; *a year later, after having received widespread criticism for her remarks, Collins told* People *magazine, "Enough has been said about this issue by people who are not knowledgeable. It should be left to doctors and politicians to discuss, not actors."*

The traditional straight fear that gayness is somehow catching has found its ideal expression in the equation of homosexuality with disease: Gay = AIDS.

> *Writer DAVID BLACK,*
> The Plague Years, *1985*

Try to spread AIDS now!

> *Attackers of a Boston man, as they shattered his jaw with a baseball bat, in a park one evening*

Killing AIDS! And when we're done with you, we're going to kill your wife and kids, just in case they've got it.

Attackers of a twenty-four-year-old Klingore, Texas man, married and with AIDS, when the man screamed, "What are you doing?!" as he was kicked and beaten

---

Plagues and epidemics like AIDS bring out the best and worst of society. Face to face with disaster and death, people are stripped down to their basic human character, to good and evil. AIDS can be a litmus test of humanity.

Philosopher JONATHAN MORENO, of George Washington University

Those who believe that AIDS is God's way of punishing sinners must be hard put to explain the deaths of so many babies who contracted the disease in the wombs of their infected mothers or of the innocent people who got it from blood transfusions. The people who think AIDS is retribution must be puzzled, too, by the disproportionate amount of talent we have lost with people who have died of AIDS. Homosexual males seem to have contributed more than their share to our culture. Frequently, the homosexual's talent is great, unique and inexplicable.

Writer and 60 Minutes *commentator ANDY ROONEY*

Wouldn't it be great if you could only get AIDS from giving money to television preachers?

Comedienne ELAYNE BOOSLER

When people in Schlafly country talk about AIDS being caused by perversion, they don't realize — and probably don't care — that they're talking about people's friends and family . . . I'm waiting for the day when one of those people says something with me in the room. They're not interested in the most effective way to fight the disease. They couldn't give a rat's ass whether or not one

million, two million or ten million gays die of AIDS. They'd probably be just as happy to put them in a camp somewhere and let
them die.

RON REAGAN

It is my hope that a cure for AIDS is not found. I also hope that it
continues to infect individuals who are sexually promiscuous and
those who share dirty needles while injecting drugs. As long as
people insist on giving this disease to themselves we should let
them do it ... AIDS could benefit us in two ways. First, by
reducing the population, and second, by lowering the birthrate
since condoms are being used extensively to prevent infection.

Reader letter to Ann Landers in August 1987;
Landers called the reader's reasoning "insane"
and warned him, "If AIDS were allowed to go
unchecked, as you hope it will be, many of your
friends, family members and colleagues would be
stricken. I promise you there would be no joy in
this world for you or for anyone else."

The planet is overpopulated, food and housing are not sufficient
— in our country also. This virus will help to kill two birds with
one stone: to get rid of the dregs of mankind and to solve a
number of vital problems.

Letter about AIDS from a twenty-six-year-old
Soviet citizen, published in a Soviet youth
newspaper in 1987

It affects homosexual men, drug users, Haitians, and hemo-
philiacs. Thank goodness it hasn't spread to human beings yet.

Caption on a 1984 political cartoon about the
general public's reaction to AIDS

Newsweek's cover story made it look like there were all these grandmothers and women with AIDS, but you opened it and you could
tell they were all queers.

MELODY PATTON, vice-president of

> *Citizens Against AIDS in School, in Arcadia,*
> *Florida, on* Newsweek's *1987 cover story*
> *featuring the photographs of hundreds of people*
> *who had died from AIDS; Patton's organization*
> *grew out of a controversy over three Arcadia boys*
> *who tested positive to the AIDS virus and who*
> *were admitted to local schools; as a result of a*
> *hate campaign, the boys and their parents were*
> *run out of town, after their house was gutted by*
> *a fire bomb*

Die, you AIDS faggots!

> *Attackers of a woman employee of the Gay and*
> *Lesbian Community Services Center of Los*
> *Angeles as they doused her with acid as she was*
> *leaving work one evening in 1985; her face,*
> *shoulders, and arms were burned in the attack.*

...the Republican party must never seem to be inciting a reaction, only responding to it. If we are low-key, logical sounding and stressing the importance of "protecting" families from the disease, then we could find ourselves in excellent shape in '88 ... Some Republicans refuse to try and exploit AIDS, but many are more than willing.

> *Republican Party consultant CHARLES*
> *RUND, in a confidential memo on how*
> *exploiting public hysteria over AIDS would help*
> *Republican Party candidates win in the 1988*
> *elections*

Nor is fearmongering solely the territory of Republicans. New York's Democratic mayor Ed Koch wanted to test all foreign visitors to the city. This is classic xenophobia — a kind of moral and medical isolationism. Perhaps Koch has never heard of the golden rule: Do unto others as you would have others do unto you. New York accounts for one-third of the AIDS cases in America. Let's cordon off the city, seal the Lincoln Tunnel, close off J.F.K. and LaGuardia and close down all road-show productions of *A Chorus*

Line. And, hey, haven't a lot of those Mets taken drugs? Fuck it; let's nuke New York. Isn't fearmongering fun?

> Editorial in *PLAYBOY* magazine,
> October 1987

———

Everyone detected with AIDS should be tattooed in the upper forearm, to protect common-needle users, and on the buttocks, to prevent the victimization of other homosexuals.

> *WILLIAM F. BUCKLEY, in a 1986*
> *editorial in* The New York Times

———

Coming from Nazi Germany and having survived Hitler and the concentration camps, I am very worried when I hear the word quarantine. Because the next thing they might decide is everyone 4'7" should be quarantined.

> *DR. RUTH WESTHEIMER, who is 4'7",*
> *on suggestions of quarantining gay men and*
> *people with AIDS*

———

How are you going to find the people to quarantine? You would have to test the entire population, 240 million people. Suppose you found three million carriers of the AIDS antibodies, what are you going to do to them? And why? And is it fair? Suppose in that group of three million you have one thousand irresponsible people who are spreading the virus; should all the others be locked up for the rest of their lives?

> *U.S. Surgeon General C. EVERETT KOOP*

———

With talk of mandatory testing we are at the point of acquiescing to the beginning of a police state. And we have to fight it. I mean, even should certain lives be endangered. We risk lives in war. That's a worthwhile war: to save our civil liberties.

> *DR. MATHILDE KRIM, co-chair of the*
> *American Foundation for AIDS Research*

———

You know, it's old hat to talk about voodoo economics, but we

Albert Gore Jr.: Not since Hoover has a president ignored reality as badly as Reagan has with AIDS.

really have a voodoo health policy. The Government's idea seems to be that if we keep sticking needles into people and taking blood tests, the disease will go away.

Former Arizona governor and presidential
candidate BRUCE BABBITT

History will deal harshly with the Reagan Administration for its failure to face up to the unprecedented threat of the AIDS epidemic. Not since Hoover has a president done less when he should have known better.

U.S. Senator ALBERT GORE JR.
(D-Tennessee)

We know that information and education about AIDS can save lives — yet this Administration has less money for mass-media information in its budget than General Secord has in his secret bank accounts. Why is President Reagan so generous with money to take lives in Central America — and yet so stingy with money

Jesse Jackson: Why does Reagan want only to preach morality against a disease that is morally indifferent?

to save lives here in the United States of America? Why is the president so reluctant to be guided by morality in his dealings with the immoral racist government of South Africa, yet wants only to preach morality in his response to this deadly disease — which is morally indifferent?

JESSE JACKSON

I came here today with the hope that this administration would do everything possible, make every resource available — there is no reason this disease cannot be conquered . . . I came here today in the hope that my epitaph would not read that I died of red tape.

ROGER LYON, a man with AIDS, testifying before Congress in 1983; Lyon died in 1984

I tried hard to keep everything going, but when I'd drive through UCLA after my [Interferon] shots, I'd break out crying . . . because I'd see all these nice-looking young men walking around

and young ladies walking around who had futures ahead of them
— and mine had been pulled out from under my feet.

> *Gay porn star BEAU MATHEWS, who was
> diagnosed with AIDS in 1984 and died in
> 1986; Mathews told one interviewer: "Why the
> hell do you think people die? They die from
> isolation! They die from being deserted."*

I hope that in my own struggle with this disease, in finally
acknowledging that I have this lethal syndrome, there might be
some measure of compassion, understanding and healing for me
and for others with it — especially those who face the disease
alone and in fear.

> *Priest and physician FATHER MICHAEL
> PETERSON, in a letter written on his death-
> bed to Catholic bishops across the United States;
> Peterson died on April 9, 1987.*

It was my position that he stayed. And if anybody felt different,
they could leave. Everybody decided it would be discrimination to
do anything else. And, anyway, we cared about him ... The
work was a way to let him know he wasn't abandoned.

> *New Orleans businesswoman DAWN
> DEDEAUX, after learning that an assistant
> editor at her publishing firm had AIDS; even
> after the employee had to quit, because he was
> no longer strong enough to come in to the office,
> Dedeaux continued sending him paychecks.*

Each one of them is Jesus in a distressing disguise.

> *MOTHER THERESA, on people with AIDS*

My gut turns over when I talk to somebody on the phone and they
die before I can even send a counselor over there. One week I had
three people die within ten days. I was just sitting in the chair
kind of vibrating. I used to cry. Now there are no more tears.

> *CHUCK JONES, intake officer at New York's*

*Gay Men's Health Crisis, Inc., a non-profit
organization providing social services to people
with AIDS*

You get the feeling you're in Beirut or on the front lines of a war.

*Manhattan physician DR. DANIEL
WILLIAM; in 1985, at the time he made the
remark, Dr. William was treating almost three
hundred people with either AIDS or AIDS-
Related Complex.*

I have a prostitute-patient with pre-AIDS and I can't get her off
the street. One day she looked especially tired. I asked her what
was wrong. She said: "I got fined $250, and now I have to go out
and work twice as hard."

*MARK KAPLAN, chief of infectious diseases
at North Shore University Hospital in Chicago*

I was driving down Santa Monica Boulevard and I saw all these
male hookers. I was tempted to yell out the window, "Hey you
guys, what the hell are you doing? This isn't a game anymore."

CHER

Two years ago, when I hosted a benefit for AIDS, I couldn't get
one major star to turn out. It ended up being just me and a transvestite onstage. I received death threats and hate mail.

JOAN RIVERS, in 1985

The number of calls I've received from the media asking for a
quote about why I'm involved in the upcoming Commitment to
Life dinner is truly amazing. I've been involved in literally dozens
of charity events for various illnesses over the years and I've never
before been asked why. I am certain that if this dinner were bene-
fiting cancer research — or any disease other than AIDS — no
one would even think of asking such a ludicrous question.

BURT REYNOLDS

Vito Russo: Why is television failing to do what it can against AIDS?

I have actress friends who are saying I won't do this or that part opposite that actor because he is gay and I don't want to get AIDS. What are we going to do? Refuse to do love scenes and play only nuns? The simple fact is that acting is the only profession where kissing is a requirement — except, of course, for prostitution.

Actress MORGAN FAIRCHILD

———

The top issue of the day is AIDS. And there has not been one major motion picture dealing exclusively with this subject. Meanwhile you turn on *Dallas* and *Dynasty* and all you get is promiscuous, indiscriminate sex with strangers. And you can't get a condom ad on network television.

VITO RUSSO

———

...our industry finds such usage of our product to be totally unacceptable ... The banana is an important product and deserves to be treated with respect and consideration ... The industry intends to hold PBS strictly responsible for any and all damages sustained through the arbitrary, capricious and totally unnecessary display of bananas in the form intended...

> *ROBERT M. MOORE, president of the International Banana Association, in a letter to PBS president Bruce Christensen protesting the use of a banana in a condom demonstration for a 1987 PBS special on AIDS*

This product has been named Ayds for more than forty-five years. Let the disease change its name.

> *FRANK DiPRIMA, executive vice president of the company that produces Ayds appetite suppressant candies, asked if the company had any plans to change its product's name*

The AIDS thing is pretty disconcerting. It means we probably can't have as much fun as bands in the past.

> *MICHAEL DIAMOND, of the group "The Beastie Boys"; one Beastie Boys' song, entitled "The New Style," contains the lyrics, "I got money and juice, twin sisters in my bed, their father had AIDS so I shot him in the head!"*

People, Andy Warhol told us, get fifteen minutes of fame. Diseases apparently get about fifteen months. Even AIDS.

> *NEWSWEEK magazine, on growing tendencies in 1987 to downplay the impact of the AIDS epidemic*

It simply became an overwhelming experience. You saw that quilt go down, and it was at dawn, and people were reading the names, and the names, and the names of all those people that have died. And all the talent gone, and the lives lost. And it simply became an overwhelming experience. It became a lot more than just my son.

> *SUE CAVES, on the spreading of the AIDS*

*quilt across the Washington Mall in October
1987; Caves lost her thirty-four-year-old son
to AIDS in 1985 and sewed a panel in his
memory for the quilt.*

———

And, at sunrise, that which Cleve Jones had first imagined some years ago, began to unfold on the Washington Mall . . . It turned out he had such a good idea. And one of the nation's oldest crafts, quilting, served the purpose it has always served — it brought folks together. It is also a good time to remind ourselves that AIDS is the *nation's* problem.

*ABC News Anchorman PETER JENNINGS,
on* ABC World News Tonight, *October 16,
1987*

———

I plan to stay with the person I'm with for years and years. I think to be gay is to be blessed. We have so much freedom, so many choices. This isn't our moment to party or to think we're going to stay young forever . . . maybe it's our time to find someone to be safe with . . . to be happy with.

Porn star KURT MARSHALL

CONVENTIONAL WISDOM

It is an odd thing, but everyone who disappears is said to be in San Francisco. It must be a delightful city and possess all the attractions of the next world.

> *OSCAR WILDE*

San Francisco may be completely gone. There may be no saving it. They even have a gay sheriff there.

> *BOB GREEN, Anita Bryant's husband,*
> *in 1977*

Homosexuality is legal in California. I'm getting out before they make it compulsory.

> *BOB HOPE*

You have to realize that all of this has been foretold centuries ago. I can't think of a more sure sign of The Final Days than having all these homosexuals parading around for their rights.

> *California Baptist minister RAY BATEMA*

I don't think homosexuality is normal behavior and I oppose the codification of gay rights. But I wouldn't harass them and I wish they could know that. Actually, I wish the whole issue could be toned down. I wish it could go away, but, of course, I know it can't.

> *GEORGE BUSH, during his campaign for the*
> *1980 Republican presidential nomination*

———

This guy wanted to know how I stood on the decriminalization of this business with consenting males. Boy, I just let him have it . . . I am not about to give in to gay liberation and codify into law the business of homosexuality . . . It is the first beginning of the breakdown of a society. It strikes at the heart of family life and I'm not about to encourage that sort of thing . . . This is the way civilizations crumble. The logical end of homosexuality is the gradual end of the human race. . .

> *U.S. Senator HENRY "SCOOP" JACKSON*
> *(1912-1983)*

———

. . . if everyone were homosexual, there would not, tomorrow, be anyone at all.

> *WILLIAM F. BUCKLEY*

———

Homosexuals or lesbians cannot produce a baby, a family or a society . . . There are no sexual preferences. The assumption that there are, is in itself a defiance of nature, creation and God.

> *AMERICAN COUNCIL OF CHRISTIAN*
> *CHURCHES, a conservative Protestant*
> *organization*

———

I don't know what the Bible says about gay people, but I do know that Jesus said go out and have children. I believe in the word of God so I went out and had ten. Could a gay couple follow the word of God like that?

> *Miami schoolteacher INEZ WILCOX, during*
> *the battle over gay rights in Dade County,*
> *Florida, in 1977*

———

My own view of sexuality is benign. Consenting sexual relations are a good thing, regardless of number, gender, or positions assumed. Incontinent baby-making is a bad thing in an over-crowded world. The muddle the Judaeo-Christian nightmare has made of our sexual attitudes is something not to be believed.

GORE VIDAL

We *have* to look on sex as something other than a way of producing offspring.

ARTHUR C. CLARKE

Observe how preoccupation with the nuclear family, and the blind faith in reproduction as the standard for sexuality, and the religious motive, tie together. Reproduction and children and the promise of an afterlife are utilized by some as magical devices to cope with the fear of death. To many, the homosexual, who does not appear to be wearing these amulets, evokes this fear.

DR. GEORGE WEINBERG, Society and the Healthy Homosexual, *1972*

Whatever it is — gay rights, women's rights, children's liberation — whenever one challenges a part of American society, one challenges all of American society. American society is repressive against gays not because it likes to repress gays for the sake of repressing gays, but because the system will crack if people begin to challenge the hypocrises and its value system.

Writer JOHN GERASSI,
author of The Boys of Boise

. . . gays are in the vanguard of that final divorce of sex from con-ventional notions of sin; the divorce of sin from mythology and religion. If we can carry this off — if we can take sex out of the realm of sin altogether and see it as something else to do with per-sonal relationships and ethics, then we can finally get around to another phase of Christianity which is long overdue. That phase is the one which deals with the question of sin as violence; sin as cruelty; sin as murder, war and starvation.

Writer ANNE RICE

Leonard Matlovich: Honored for killing and discharged for loving.

This is a society that does tragic things, obscene things; yet it is only the physical relations between human beings — the sexual relations — that we seem to term obscene.

MALCOLM BOYD

The Air Force pinned a medal on me for killing a man and discharged me for making love to one.

Former Air Force sergeant LEONARD MATLOVICH (1943-1988), who, in 1975, set himself up as a test case to challenge the U.S. military's policy of automatically discharging homosexuals.

It is better to control a restrictive and hostile emotion . . . than a generous and expansive emotion such as love. Conventional morality has erred, not in demanding self-control, but in demanding it in the wrong place.

Philosopher BERTRAND RUSSELL (1870-1972)

It's a much more honorable act to rim a total stranger than it is to deny a poor woman an abortion, and it's much more righteous to help an underage lesbian sneak into the bar than it is to force her to pray in school.

Writer PAT CALIFIA, in a 1981 article on gay liberation.

You people are a ploy for Communist Russia to destroy the United States and you don't even realize it. You'll allow anarchy and immorality to abound, acts of sexual deviancy will flourish ... God will destroy us as He has other promiscuous civilizations like Sodom and Gomorrah. Or we'll be in bondage by Communist Russia.

REV. DAN C. FORE, head of the New York State chapter of the Moral Majority, in an interview with The Advocate.

... those who behave in a homosexual fashion ... shall not enter the kingdom of God.

POPE JOHN PAUL II, in his 1986 Letter to the Bishops of the Catholic Church on the Pastoral Care of Homosexual Persons.

You know, God's kingdom, or Jesus' kingdom is for everybody. It's not reserved for pious heterosexual hypocrites. After all, Jesus was really one of the first social radicals. He didn't appeal to the "respectable" people of his time ... He ministered largely to outcasts.

JAMES PURDY

The purpose is to say to all citizens that God accepts you as is, and you don't have ... to conform to some obsolete, obsessive-compulsive, medieval, semi-psychotic world view.

Attorney JOHN WAHL, who helped organize demonstrations to protest the pope's visit to San Francisco in the fall of 1987.

I find it difficult to believe that a church that blesses dogs in a Virginia fox hunt can't find a way to bless life-giving, lasting relationships between human beings.

> *JOHN SPONG, Episcopal Bishop of Newark, New Jersey; in 1988, Spong's diocese became the first in the nation to publicly support ministers who encourage and bless committed gay relationships.*

———

Homosexual affection can be as selfless as heterosexual affection, and therefore we cannot see that it is in some way morally wrong. An act which expresses true affection between two individuals and gives pleasure to them both does not seem to us to be sinful simply because it is homosexual.

> TOWARDS A QUAKER VIEW OF SEX, *1964*

———

There will be no satanic churches, no more free distribution of pornography, no more abortion on demand, no more talk of rights for homosexuals. When the Christian majority takes control, pluralism will be seen as evil and the state will not allow anybody the right to practice evil.

> *GARY POTTER, Catholics for Christian Political Action*

———

They should be killed through government means. There are a lot of people in Watertown that enjoy living in a non-Christian world and it's got to be stopped.

> *REV. DANIEL LOVELY, of the Watertown Baptist Temple in New York, advocating capital punishment for homosexuals.*

———

I have never come across anyone in whom the moral sense was dominant who was not heartless, cruel, vindictive, log-stupid, and entirely lacking in the smallest sense of humanity.

> *OSCAR WILDE*

Of all tyrannies, a tyranny exercised for the good of its victims may be the most oppressive. It may be better to live under robber barons than under omnipotent moral busybodies. The robber baron's cruelty may sometimes sleep, his cupidity may at some point be satiated; but those who torment us for our own good will torment us without end for they do so with the approval of their own conscience...

C.S. LEWIS

He who wears his morality but as his best garment were better naked.

KAHLIL GIBRAN (1883-1931),
The Prophet, *1923*

As to the Reverend Falwell: If he thinks that I'm a Communist plot to subvert the youth of Western society, what is he — a strong believer in democracy? Or does he have his own brand of Communist policies that prevent anyone who doesn't follow his beliefs from breathing God's free air? It's funny that the Russians also think that Boy George and Michael Jackson are Western society's way of subverting their youth.

BOY GEORGE

I learned that boys no longer kiss girls without first having gone before the mayor; that homosexuals are mending their ways by reading Marx in concentration camps; that taxis must be lit up at night so as not to harbor sin; that the bedsheets of Red Army soldiers are inspected in order to shame those who masturbate; that children have no need for sex education because they never think about dirty things like that ... that it is unhealthy for people to enjoy themselves sexually without reproducing.

French writer PIERRE HERBART, in his diary, during a tour of the Soviet Union with Andre Gide in 1935.

When you're gay you live in constant fear which eventually becomes paranoia because you know you can't really trust anyone. At any moment anyone can accuse you of being homosexual, which means immediate dismissal from the School of Medicine, being branded by the system for life, perhaps prison at some point ... If you are seen holding hands with someone of your gender, you could be put in jail for at least one year. I have friends in jail now for that reason.

> *EDUARDO, a gay Cuban refugee,*
> *on life in Cuba.*

––––––

If anyone wants to engage in any kind of sexual activity with any consenting partner, that is their business ... I don't feel that legality should have anything to do with it. There are certain bodily functions of mine which I will not allow to be supervised.

> *Atheist activist MADALYN MURRAY*
> *O'HAIR, in a 1965 interview*

––––––

Even if, for the sake of argument, we allow that "drink, gambling, and immorality" are physically and/or mentally injurious, it is of the essence of a free country that the community will take the risk of letting anyone go to hell in his own way, provided he does no direct violence to others.

> *ALAN WATTS*

––––––

There must be a realm of private morality and immorality which is, in brief and crude terms, not the law's business.

> *From "The Wolfenden Report," a 1957 govern-*
> *ment study in Great Britain which recommended*
> *that public statutes should not legislate morality*
> *and that homosexual acts between consenting*
> *adults in private be decriminalized; most of the*
> *report's recommendations were implemented in*
> *1967.*

––––––

Sodomy was a criminal offense at common law and was forbidden by the laws of the original thirteen states when they ratified the Bill of Rights. In 1868, when the 14th Amendment was ratified, all but five of the thirty-seven states in the Union had criminal sodomy laws. In fact, until 1961, all fifty states outlawed sodomy, and today, twenty-four states and the District of Columbia continue to provide criminal penalties for sodomy performed in private and between consenting adults. Against this background, to claim that a right to engage in such conduct is "deeply rooted in this nation's history and tradition" or "implicit in the concept of ordered liberty" is, at best, facetious.

> *Supreme Court Justice BYRON WHITE,*
> *writing for the high court's majority, which*
> *upheld the constitutionality of Georgia's sodomy*
> *laws in 1986.*

Isn't it a violation of the Georgia sodomy law for the Supreme Court to have its head up its ass?

> *Reader letter to* Playboy *magazine,*
> *February 1987*

The Reagan Administration has fostered a climate in which a barest majority of the Supreme Court caters to the passions and hatreds of the American mob, stripping away the constitutional shield outside our bedrooms ... How tragically ironic that an Administration that promised to get Government "off our backs" is now so active in draping Government gumshoes over every part of our anatomies.

> *Columnist CARL T. ROWAN*

Why is it that the people most outraged when government puts its hand in your pocket for taxes are often the people quickest to applaud when government sticks its nose into your bedroom?

> NEW YORK TIMES *editorial, commenting*
> *on the Supreme Court decision upholding the*
> *constitutionality of Georgia's sodomy laws.*

We protect those rights not because they contribute, in some direct and material way, to the general public welfare, but because they form so central a part of an individual's life ... The

Byron White: privacy for consenting adults is "facetious."

fact that individuals define themselves in a significant way through their intimate sexual relationships with others suggests, in a nation as diverse as ours, that there may be many "right" ways of conducting those relationships, and that much of the richness of a relationship will come from the freedom an individual has to choose the form and nature of these intensely personal bonds.

Supreme Court Justice HARRY BLACKMUN, dissenting from the high court's majority, in the 1986 decision to uphold the constitutionality of Georgia's sodomy laws.

We confess to a strong personal prejudice in favor of the boy-girl variety of sex, but our belief in a free, rational and humane society demands a tolerance of those whose sexual inclinations are different from our own ... Society benefits as much from the differences in men as from their similarities, and we should create a culture that not only accepts these differences, but respects and actually nurtures them.

HUGH HEFNER, elaborating "The Playboy Philosophy," in Playboy *magazine in the early 1950s.*

———

Irregular — unnatural — call them by what names of reproach you will, of these gratifications nothing but good, pure good, if pleasure without pain be a pure good ... But when the act be pure good, punishment for whatsoever *purpose*, from whatever *source*, in whatsoever *name* and in whatsoever *degree* ... will be not only evil, but so much pure evil.

English philosopher JEREMY BENTHAM (1748-1832), founder of utilitarianism, on homosexuality.

———

Whatever crushes individuality is despotism, by whatever name it may be called.

English philosopher JOHN STUART MILL (1806-1873)

PASSION

I believe the nearest I have come to perfect love was with a young coal miner when I was about sixteen.

> *D.H. LAWRENCE; Lawrence's close friend and biographer Richard Aldington once remarked, "I should say Lawrence was about eighty-five percent hetero and fifteen percent homo."*

Natalie, my husband kisses your hands, and I the rest.

> *French writer COLETTE, in a note to the well-known lesbian Natalie Barney; Colette eventually left her husband, not for Natalie Barney, but for an aristocratic lesbian, the Marquise de Belbouef.*

Do you imagine that your life with others will be happier than it is with me? Of course it won't be happier. You're only free with me ... I'm now clear in my mind that I do love you: if you won't come back or let me join you, you're committing a crime. *Remember what you were before you knew me.*

> *ARTHUR RIMBAUD (1854-1891), to poet Paul Verlaine*

I am having a bad dream. I'll come back someday.

> *PAUL VERLAINE (1844-1896), in a letter*
> *to his wife from Brussels, where he had run off*
> *with Arthur Rimbaud.*

———

Darling, you're divine. I've had an affair with your husband.
You'll be next.

> *TALLULAH BANKHEAD, to Joan*
> *Crawford; Crawford was married at the time to*
> *Douglas Fairbanks Jr. and supposedly replied,*
> *"I'm so sorry, Miss Bankhead, but I just love*
> *men."*

———

Though I have been in love a good many times I have never experienced the bliss of requited love. I have most loved people who cared little or nothing for me.

> *W. SOMERSET MAUGHAM*

———

...I have slain lions and terrified captains; but now
I am the slave of a boy, glancing like a young deer ...
I would bow myself before him, if Allah existed not,
    saying—
You are my God!

> *Turkish sultan SELIM I (1476-1520)*

———

Up from the earth I rose with his wings,
And death itself I could have found sweet.

> *MICHELANGELO, from a sonnet to Febo di*
> *Poggio, a young male prostitute who worked as*
> *one of his models.*

———

All my life I have had a recurring dream. I dream I am on a train rolling north along the river. Next to me is a large, burly sort of man, a detective. I am manacled to this man and I know I am on my way to Sing Sing, *and I am the happiest man that ever lived.*

> *Theater critic and radio commentator*
> *ALEXANDER WOOLLCOTT*

*(1887-1943); Woollcott, who enjoyed dressing
as a woman in college and who once confided to
playwright Anita Loos that he had always
wanted to be a girl, was troubled much of his
life by confused sexual feelings.*

———

But I, to grace the goddess, like wax of the sacred bees when smitten by the sun, am melted when I look at the young limbs of boys.
Greek poet PINDAR (522-443 B.C.)

———

Oh my dear sir, if you knew how little I care for your sex, you wouldn't get any ideas in your head. The fact is, in the way of males, I like only the bulls I paint.
*French painter ROSA BONHEUR
(1822-1899), to a man who teased her about
going out in society unchaperoned; Bonheur, one
of the most distinguished animal painters in
history, lived with one female lover, Nathalie
Micas, for over forty years. When Nathalie
died, an American painter, Anna Klumpke,
moved into the house and stayed with Bonheur
for the next seven years, until Bonheur's death at
the age of seventy-seven; Bonheur lies buried in
a vault that includes both Micas and Klumpke.*

———

I like homosexuality where the lovers are friends all their lives, and there are many lovers and many friends.
Poet ALLEN GINSBERG

———

I have even found someone with whom I can speak of love: a good-looking, blond young Roman of sixteen, half a head taller than I am. But I see him only once a week, when he dines with me on Sunday evening.
*German archaeologist JOHANN JOACHIM
WINCKELMANN (1717-1768), during a
trip through Italy; Winckelmann was murdered
in 1768 by a young ex-convict he took back to
his hotel room in Trieste.*

Peter Ilyich Tchaikovsky:
Indescribably fascinated.

. . . in this romantic, anachronistic life the ambassador is a bosom friend of the felon; the prince, with a certain independence of action with which his aristocratic breeding has furnished him . . . on leaving the duchess's party goes off to confer in private with the hooligan . . .

> *MARCEL PROUST (1871-1922), on homosexuality;* Cities of the Plain, *1922*

———

I want to love a strong young man of the lower classes and be loved by him, and even hurt by him.

> *E.M. FORSTER*

———

Bob will finally drive me simply crazy with his indescribable fascination . . . I begin to crave Bob and get lonely without him . . . Frightful how I love him!

> *Russian composer PETER ILYICH*

*TCHAIKOVSKY (1840-1893), writing in
his diary about his teenaged nephew, Vladimir
Davidov, nicknamed "Bob" by the family;
Tchaikovsky eventually dedicated his Sixth
Symphony, the* Pathetique, *to him.*

You rest your magnificent ass against the wall, Cyris. Why give such pleasure to the stone, which is oblivious?

Greek poet STRATO (c. A.D. 1st century)

O boy, so long as thy chin remains smooth, never will I cease from fawning, no, not if it doomed for me to die.

Greek poet THEOGNIS (600-540 B.C.)

How could you know, O possibly know,
That the reins of my soul are in your hands!

Greek poet IBYCUS (570-525 B.C.)

How idiotic people are when they are in love. What an age-old devastating disease!

NOEL COWARD

To be in love is merely to be in a state of perceptual anaesthesia — to mistake an ordinary young man for a Greek god or an ordinary young woman for a goddess.

Journalist H.L. MENCKEN (1880-1956)

Love him ... love him and let him love you. Do you think anything else under heaven really matters?

JAMES BALDWIN, Giovanni's Room, *1956*

At one moment with my cock in his arse, the image was, and as I write still is, overpoweringly erotic, and I reflect that whatever the

Sunday papers have said about *Crimes of Passion* was of little or no importance compared with this.

> *JOE ORTON, vacationing in Tangier, while in London his play* Crimes of Passion *was receiving mixed reviews.*

————

I thought of you again in the Arenes at Nimes, and under the arches of the Pont du Gard; that is to say that, in these places, I desired you with a strange appetite; for, far from each other, there is something lost in us, something incomplete.

> *French writer GUSTAVE FLAUBERT (1821-1880), to friend Alfred Le Poittevin; Poittevin once wrote Flaubert, "We are something like one single man, and we live of the same life." Flaubert was thrown into a rage when Poittevin married in 1846: "I experienced, when he married, a very deep stab of jealousy. . . ."*

————

Certainly our own day overemphasizes sexuality as the cause of behaviour and emotion, but conversely many Victorians managed what seems to us the difficult balancing act of believing that love between men which had no overt physical consequences was therefore untouched by physical motivation.

> *Writer ROBERT BERNARD MARTIN*

————

I am neither a god nor an angel but a man like any other, and confess to loving those dear to me more than other men. You may be sure that I love the Earl of Buckingham more than anyone else . . . Christ had his John, and I have my Steenie.

> *JAMES I (1566-1625), king of England, in a letter about his favorite, the Earl of Buckingham, nicknamed "Steenie" by the king.*

————

I could love anything on earth that appeared to wish it.

> *LORD BYRON (1788-1824)*

Eleanor Roosevelt: Her love affair with Lorena Hickok remained secret for years.

I've been trying today to bring back your face — to remember just *how* you look ... Most clearly I remember your eyes, with a kind of teasing smile in them, and the feeling of that soft spot just northeast of the corner of your mouth against my lips ... Goodnight, dear one. I want to put my arms around you and kiss you at the corner of your mouth. And in a little more than a week now — I shall!

Journalist LORENA HICKOK (1892-1968), to Eleanor Roosevelt. Hickok was a reporter when she first met Mrs. Roosevelt; their relationship deepened, and shortly after becoming First Lady, Eleanor had her moved into the White House, where Lorena secretly lived for four years. In a 1933 letter to Hickok, Eleanor wrote: "Hick darling. All day I've thought of you and another birthday I will be with you ... Oh! I want to put my arms around you, I ache to hold you close. Your ring is a great comfort. I look at it and think she does love me or I wouldn't be wearing it!"

The mightiest kings have had their minions —
Great Alexander lov'd Hephestion;
The conquering Hector for Hylas wept;
And for Patroclus stern Achilles droop'd.
And not kings only but the wisest men —
The Roman Tully lov'd Octavius;
Grave Socrates wild Alcibiades.

> *CHRISTOPHER MARLOWE*
> *(1564-1593),* Edward II, *1590*

———

Thy love to me was wonderful, passing the love of women.

> *DAVID's lament over Jonathan,*
> *in the Bible (II Sam. 1:26)*

———

Some people meet and part ways, others bond together on a life-long stream. I guess you could call our relationship destiny.

> *Film producer ISMAIL MERCHANT, on his*
> *twenty-eight-year relationship with director*
> *James Ivory; Merchant and Ivory have been*
> *responsible for such widely acclaimed films as* A
> Room With a View *and* Maurice.

———

. . .[on the telephone] our friends often think I'm Don and vice versa. When we're working on something together we sometimes use a tape recorder, and it's the most extraordinary thing. Even we can't tell the voices apart! That's what twenty-six years have done.

> *CHRISTOPHER ISHERWOOD, on his*
> *relationship with artist Don Bachardy; Isher-*
> *wood and Bachardy were together for thirty-two*
> *years, until Isherwood's death in 1986*

———

On one occasion he was standing at the door of our cottage, looking down the garden brilliant in the sun, when a missionary sort of man arrived with a tract and wanted to put it in his hand. "Keep your tract," said George. "I don't want it." "But don't you wish to know the way to heaven?" said the man. "No, I don't," was the reply, "can you see that *we're in heaven here* — we don't *want* any better than this, so go away!" And the man turned and fled.

> *Victorian writer and social activist EDWARD CARPENTER (1844-1929), writing of his lover of thirty years, George Merrill; "Thus, we settled down, two bachelors," Carpenter wrote in his autobiography. "Our lives had become necessary to each other so that what anyone said was of little importance." Merrill died in 1928, Carpenter less than a year later.*

———

It is not my habit to write to papers after reading reviews of my books. But after coming across the one by Martha Duffy on my novel *The Eye of the Storm*, in which she refers to me as "living in Sydney with several dogs and a male housekeeper," I feel I must draw your attention to an incorrect, and I should have thought gratuitous, biographical detail. The distinguished and universally respected man who has given me his friendship and moral support over a period of thirty-four years, has never been a housekeeper. *I* am that, and shall continue playing the role at least till I am paralyzed; it keeps me in touch with reality.

> *Novelist PATRICK WHITE, in a 1974 letter to* Time *magazine*

———

I *sleep* with Mr. Williams.

> *FRANK MERLO (1922-1963), secretary and lover to Tennessee Williams, when asked by Hollywood mogul Jack Warner at dinner one night, "And what do* you *do, young man?"*

———

When he died, I went to pieces. I retreated into a shell. For nine months, I wouldn't speak to a living soul. I just clammed up. I wouldn't answer the telephone and I wouldn't leave the house.

> *TENNESSEE WILLIAMS, on the death of his lover Frank Merlo, from lung cancer, in 1963.*

Do not be so reserved; I have become yours so completely that nothing of myself is left. You know my weakness: when it has no one to lean upon, it drives me to despair of life.

> *Dutch humanist ERASMUS (1466-1536), to*
> *a beloved male friend*

...and I honestly wish I were dead.

> *SAPPHO (c. 6th century B.C.), in a poem*
> *written on the departure of a beloved girl, Atthis*

We'd faced up to what was going to come a good deal earlier than this, and he was not in any terror of dying. Not at all. I mean, I don't think he really had any particular conviction as to what was going to happen after that, but he was certainly not afraid of dying. And he died — in my arms, in fact — peacefully, as far as he could be said to be peaceful when he in fact was very ill . . . But what was his greatest feeling was sadness and sorrow at the thought of leaving me, his friends, and his responsibilities. He'd always said earlier, to me, "I must die first, before you, because I don't know what I would do without you."

> *English tenor PETER PEARS (1910-1986),*
> *describing the death of his lover, British*
> *composer Benjamin Britten. Britten died on*
> *December 4, 1976; he and Pears had been*
> *lovers for forty years.*

And now she is in the vault at the American Cathedral on the Quay d'Orsay — and I'm here alone. And nothing more — only what was. You will know that nothing is very clear with me — everything is empty and blurred.

> *ALICE B. TOKLAS (1877-1967), in a letter*
> *written to friends four days after the death of her*
> *lover, Gertrude Stein, in 1946. A little more*
> *than a year after Stein's death, Toklas wrote*
> *another friend: "I wish to God we had gone*
> *together as I always so fatuously thought we*

Composer Benjamin Britten: He and tenor Peter Pears were lovers for forty years.

would — a bomb — a shipwreck — just anything but this."

———

This isn't just pain, it is torture ... My God, if it weren't for a stubborn instructive holding to a faith that is in me ... that we shall, we *must* meet again, I wouldn't endure this thing another hour...

LADY UNA TROUBRIDGE (1887-1963), in her diary, after the death of her lover, Radclyffe Hall, in 1943. Hall's epitaph reads: "And if God Choose, I Shall But Love Thee Better After Death. Una."

Wail for me, Antilochus, rather than for the dead man — for me, Achilles, who still lives.

Achilles' lament for Patroclus, from
AESCHYLUS' play The Myrmidons
(c. 475 B.C.)

On this holy spot, sacred to Zeus, Krion has consummated his union with the son of Bathycles and, proclaiming it proudly to the world, dedicates to it this imperishable memorial...

Ancient Greek graffito (c. 650 B.C.),
chiseled at a site near Thebes

OF HISTORICAL INTEREST

There have been clever warriors amongst the homosexuals —
Alcibiades, Caesar, Peter the Great and many Turkish sultans,
whose names I forget — but never a diplomat of distinction.

OTTO VON BISMARCK (1815-1898),
founder and first chancellor of the German
Empire

———

Homosexuality between men, though not between women, is illegal in England . . . Every person who has taken the trouble to
study the subject knows that this law is the effect of a barbarous
and ignorant superstition in favour of which no rational argument
of any sort of kind can be advanced.

BERTRAND RUSSELL, in 1929

———

In addition to the normal sexual urge in men and women, Nature
in her sovereign mood had endowed at birth certain male and
female individuals with the homosexual urge, thus placing them
in a sexual bondage which renders them physically and psychically incapable — even with the best intention — of normal erection. This urge creates in advance a direct horror of the opposite
sex, and the victim of this passion finds it impossible to suppress
the feeling which individuals of his own sex exercise upon him.

Hungarian physician KARL MARIA

KERTBENY (1824-1882), in the first appearance of the word "homosexual," which Kertbeny coined, in an 1869 pamphlet calling for the repeal of laws persecuting homosexuals.

———

Once, a philosopher; twice, a sodomite!

VOLTAIRE, to a friend who had "experimented" with homosexuality once and desired to try it again; Voltaire himself acknowledged having once had a homosexual encounter; in other versions of the story, Voltaire made the remark to Frederick the Great.

———

My veneration for you has something of the nature of a "religious crush" because of its undeniable erotic undertone. This abominable feeling comes from the fact that as a boy I was the victim of a sexual assault by a man I once worshipped.

Psychologist CARL JUNG (1875-1961), in a letter to Sigmund Freud; both Jung and Freud acknowledged the homosexual overtones in their friendship.

———

And so what I seem to be afraid of is the voice of the world — an estimable place — the voice one thinks of as gossip although it has a true tidal force. Have you heard? Old Cheever, crowding seventy, has gone Gay. Old Cheever has come out of the closet. Old Cheever has run off to Bessarabia with a hairy youth half his age.

Writer JOHN CHEEVER (1912-1983), in his private journal, after falling in love and beginning a homosexual relationship with a young writer

———

. . . my father was bisexual; he had this tremendous sexual ambivalence. He spent an incredible amount of energy creating this totally masculine, martini-mixing, dog-breeding, duck-hunting father of three — the beautiful wife, the whole American masculine patrician dream. Then he got to a point in his life where he realized that it was pointless. Why cover it up? He was who he was.

> *SUSAN CHEEVER, daughter of John*
> *Cheever and author of* Home Before Dark,
> *a biographical memoir in which she candidly*
> *discussed her father's sexuality.*

———

I thought that men like that shot themselves.

> *KING GEORGE V (1865-1936), of*
> *England, when told that a man he knew was*
> *homosexual*

———

Every woman's husband, and every man's wife.

> *Popular Roman epithet for Julius Caesar*
> *(102-44 B.C.); Caesar was also publicly*
> *disparaged as "the Queen of Bithynia," as the*
> *result of scandal arising from his alleged sexual*
> *involvement with the king of Bithynia, when*
> *Caesar was a young aide to that country.*

———

Elizabeth was King, now James will be Queen!

> *Popular chant when James I ascended to the*
> *throne of England after the death of Elizabeth I*
> *in 1603; some historians have recorded the*
> *chant as, "The King is dead, long live the*
> *Queen!" James' homosexuality was widely*
> *known among his contemporaries.*

———

Really ... What could possibly be more harmless? Everybody knows what Jimmy is. Why, his friends call me the Queen of the Fairies!

> *WALLIS SIMPSON, the Duchess of Windsor*
> *(1897-1986), protesting her husband's objec-*
> *tions to her being seen in public so often with*
> *a well-known gay man, Jimmy Donahue,*
> *the Woolworth's heir*

Herman Melville: A honeymoon for Ishmael and Queequeg.

The nearest I ever came to leaving you was when you told me you thought I was a fairy in the Rue Palatine...

> *F. SCOTT FITZGERALD, to his wife, Zelda; Zelda accused him of having a homosexual relationship with Ernest Hemingway; "I really loved him," Fitzgerald once wrote of Hemingway, "but of course it wore out like a love affair. The fairies have spoiled all that"; Fitzgerald partly blamed the dissolution of his friendship with Hemingway on gossip, allegedly spread by homosexuals, that he and Hemingway were lovers.*

They tell me that Mr. Hemingway usually kicks people like me in the crotch.

> *TENNESSEE WILLIAMS, when critic Kenneth Tynan offered to introduce him to Hemingway in 1959*

Gertrude Stein and me are just like brothers.
> *ERNEST HEMINGWAY, in a letter to*
> *writer Sherwood Anderson*

———

I found Queequeg's arm thrown over me in the most loving and affectionate manner. You had almost thought I had been his wife ... Thus, then in our heart's honeymoon, lay I and Queequeg — a cozy, loving pair ... He pressed his forehead against mine, clasped me around the waist, and said that henceforth we were married.
> *Ishmael, in HERMAN MELVILLE's*
> Moby Dick, *1851*

———

So far as I know, nothing of the kind has ever been attempted before in fiction. Hitherto the subject has either been treated as pornography or introduced as an episode ... I have treated it as a fact of nature — a simple, though at present tragic, fact. I have written the life of a woman who is a born invert...
> *RADCLYFFE HALL, in a letter to her*
> *publisher; the letter accompanied the manuscript*
> *of her novel* The Well of Loneliness.

———

I say deliberately that this novel is not fit to be sold by any bookseller or to be borrowed from any library ... I would rather give a healthy boy or a healthy girl a phial of prussic acid than this novel. Poison kills the body, but moral poison kills the soul.
> *Critic JAMES DOUGLAS, in a 1928 review*
> *of* The Well of Loneliness *in the London*
> Sunday Express; *Douglas' review inadver-*
> *tently prompted an avalanche of sales of the book*
> *in London bookstores.*

———

Ancient writers over a period of time, having a large volume of her work in front of them, alleged that Sappho was addicted to Lesbianism. It must be admitted that her poetry shows that she entertained emotions stronger than mere friendship toward other women, but in the extant remains there is not a word to connect herself or her companions with homosexual practices and very little — but that decisive enough — to show her awareness of their existence.

> *From the 1974 Encylopaedia Britannica entry on Sappho; the existing fragments of Sappho's poetry, which the Encyclopaedia found "decisive enough," amount to barely seven hundred lines — about five percent of her original work.*

Sappho wrote only of one theme, sang it, laughed it, sighed it, wept it, sobbed it . . . a song of love.

> *WILLA CATHER (1876-1947)*

Let us remember this event and this man. He is too precious to die. Let us repair, once a year, to our accustomed houses of worship and there give thanks to God that one day in 1865 brought together the greatest poet America has ever produced and the damndest ass.

> *H.L. MENCKEN, on Secretary of the Interior James Harlan, who fired poet Walt Whitman from his job at the Department of the Interior in 1865 after learning that Whitman was the author of* Leaves of Grass

Some of his poems are among the most cynical instances of indecent exposure I recollect, outside what is sold as obscene literature.

> *OLIVER WENDELL HOLMES (1809-1894), on Walt Whitman's* Leaves of Grass

There is no one in this great wide world of America whom I love and honor so much.

> *OSCAR WILDE, in a note to Walt Whitman*

I've gotten a lot of criticism about not showing homosexuals in

Oliver Wendell Holmes: He
was offended by *Leaves of
Grass* — or perhaps he was
explaining that he liked it.

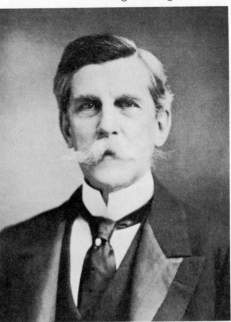

their best light or having a happy ending. I hope there are happy
homosexuals — they just don't happen to be at this party.

> *MART CROWLEY, defending his play* The
> Boys in the Band, *in a 1969 interview;
> when director William Friedkin made a film
> of the play two years later, Friedkin adopted
> Crowley's line of defense almost word-for-word.
> "I hope there are happy homosexuals," Friedkin
> told one interviewer. "There just don't happen
> to be any in my film."*

In the theatre, *The Boys in the Band* was a conventional play . . . It
was like *The Women*, but with a forties-movie bomber-crew cast: a
Catholic, a Jew, a Negro, a butch faggot, a nellie faggot, a
hustler, and so on . . . The fun of the faggot vernacular and the
interaction of the troupe of actors onstage helped a little to conceal
the play's mechanics. . .

> *From PAULINE KAEL's review of the movie*
> The Boys in the Band, *as the review*

originally appeared in The New Yorker,
March 21, 1970

———

In the theatre, *The Boys in the Band* was a conventional play . . . It
was like *The Women*, but with a forties-movie bomber-crew cast: a
Catholic, a Jew, a Negro, one butch type, one nellie, a hustler,
and so on . . . The fun of the homosexual vernacular and the
interaction of the troupe of actors onstage helped a little to conceal
the play's mechanics . . .

From PAULINE KAEL's review of the movie
The Boys in the Band, *as it appeared three
years later — with all of the "faggot" references
removed — in her collection* Deeper Into
Movies

———

There will be killings. The film will increase the hostility toward
gays and give people ideas on how to act out that hostility.

*ARTHUR BELL, in an editorial on William
Friedkin's 1980 film* Cruising

———

There are *always* dangers in democracy. Freedom of speech will
always allow those who hold heinous and repugnant points of view
to speak out. And the very same argument now given by some
gays — that *Cruising* is a clear danger to the public welfare —
could someday be turned around by Christian fundamentalists,
with disastrous results for gay people. If one group is muzzled,
who knows which will be next to feel the censor's gag? Today
Cruising, tomorrow perhaps *Word Is Out*.

1980 editorial in THE ADVOCATE, *on
the demands of some gay activists that the
distribution and exhibition of William
Friedkin's film* Cruising *be stopped*

———

Would you be surprised to know that this rough tough individual
was wearing pink satin undies under his rough exterior clothing?
He is. This person is a transvestite: a man who is more comfort-

able wearing girls' clothes. One might say, there but for the grace
of God go I.

From the narration of the 1953 film Glen or
Glenda?, *a pseudo-documentary about trans-
vestism that one critic has said "could well be
the worst movie ever made." In another scene,
the film's protagonist is seen spending a troubled
evening with his girlfriend, as the narrator
solemnly informs us: "His hands move to caress
the smooth material of her angora sweater —
which he has so longed and so desperately
wanted to put on his own body."*

Beneath the duality of sex there is a oneness. Every male is potentially a female and every female potentially a male. If a man
wants to understand a woman, he must discover the woman in
himself, and if a woman would understand a man, she must dig in
her own consciousness to discover her own maculine traits.

Sexologist and early homosexual rights activist
MAGNUS HIRSCHFELD (1868-1935)

All they that love not tobacco and boys are fools.

Attributed to CHRISTOPHER MARLOWE

He's mad that trusts in the tameness of a wolf, a horse's health, a
boy's love, or a whore's oath.

WILLIAM SHAKESPEARE (1564-1616),
King Lear *(Act III, Scene 6)*

. . .if any device could be found whereby a state or an army was
made up only of lovers and beloved, there would be no better way
of living, since lovers would abstain from all ugly things and
would be ambitious in pursuing honor and truth towards each
other; and in battle side by side, such troops, although few, would
conquer most of the world, since a man would be less willing to be
seen by his beloved than by all the rest of the world, fleeing the
ranks during a fight or throwing away his arms; he would choose

to die many times rather than that; yes, and as to deserting his beloved, or refusing to aid him in times of peril, no one is so base that Love itself would not inspire him to valour and make of him the born hero.

From the speech of Phaidros, in PLATO's Symposium *(c. 384 B.C.)*

I dig beautiful Oriental men. Asking me to shoot at them is the same thing as asking heterosexual soldiers to shoot at beautiful young girls they'd like to fuck!

Writer DON JACKSON, writing about the Vietnam War in Gay Power *in 1970*

SOLDIERS: MAKE EACH OTHER, NOT WAR!

Anti-Vietnam War poster at a 1969 rally in San Francisco

The heinous conduct of the people of Sodom is extraordinary, in as much as they departed from the natural passion and longing of the male for the female, which was implanted by God, and desired what is altogether contrary to nature. Whence comes this perversity? Undoubtedly from Satan...

MARTIN LUTHER (1483-1546)

...because of such crimes there are famines, earthquakes, and pestilences...

Byzantine Emperor JUSTINIAN (A.D. 483-565), in an edict calling for the repentance of homosexuals

Several people who I've talked to who were there claim ... the person who probably started the Stonewall Riot was a Puerto Rican, a very macho-looking young Puerto Rican guy who may not even have been gay. Who provoked people and who kept shouting, "What's the matter with you faggots, why don't you get in there and get those cops — why do you let them get away with this, stop letting them beat you up!" And three hundred people, who I trust as accurate reporters, say he was the one who threw the first stone and provoked everyone else into doing it, and that they are not at all convinced he was even gay.

Gay activist BRUCE VOELLER

———

Much has been written regarding the fact that the Stonewall Riots occurred only days after [Judy Garland's] death, and that the queens were the ones who turned on the police and said NO, NOT THIS TIME ... Judy's death inspired those Stonewall queens.

Writer GREGG HOWE

———

He just kind of smirked, as if to say, "Too bad," and then I got all flushed and hot, and I shot him.

From the police confession of DAN WHITE, former policeman and former San Francisco city supervisor who shot and killed gay city supervisor Harvey Milk and San Francisco mayor George Moscone. According to his confession, White only went to see Milk to ask for his old job on the board of supervisors back; Milk's alleged reaction infuriated him.

———

Dan White may have pulled the trigger, but Anita Bryant and John Briggs loaded the gun.

ROBIN TYLER

———

The jury, as Dan White's attorney had requested, convicted Dan White on two counts of voluntary manslaughter, for which he will serve a few years — after which he can look forward to cops buying him drinks for the rest of his life.

Writer GREIL MARCUS, in a commentary on the Dan White trial, in Rolling Stone *magazine*

Sara Jane Moore got life for *missing* Gerald Ford.

> *Spectator at Dan White's trial; White claimed,*
> *in part, that eating too much junk food had*
> *impaired his thinking at the time he shot Harvey*
> *Milk and George Moscone; he received a max-*
> *imum sentence of seven years and eight months*
> *for the murders; his lenient sentence provoked a*
> *riot at City Hall. Ironically, White had*
> *previously been a strong proponent of the death*
> *penalty, especially in cases involving the murder*
> *of public figures. White served five and a half*
> *years of his sentence. He committed suicide*
> *shortly after his parole.*

While we were watching a training film of the Dan White riot at City Hall, officers threw things at the TV screen and shouted, "Kill the faggots!"

> *Former San Francisco police officer P.*
> *THOMAS CARY*

I'm going to make Attila the Hun look like a faggot.

> *Former Philadelphia mayor FRANK RIZZO*

If through Gay Games and the Procession of the Arts we can characterize our own culture as one of tolerance and understanding, then we have a vehicle through which we can begin to teach others.

> *Olympic athlete TOM WADDELL*
> *(1937-1987), founder of the Gay Games*

LOOSE ENDS

Homosexuality is not all self-hate, or guilt feelings, or love, or domination or submission, or any one thing; it's a many-branching path, down which we are all walking.

SAMUEL STEWARD

Marriage is open to all men, but the love of boys to philosophers only.

Greek writer LUCIAN (c. A.D. 150)

In a healthy society, [homosexuality] will be contained, segregated, controlled, and stigmatized, carrying both a legal and a social sanction.

PATRICK BUCHANAN

I've always had a funny feeling about Pat's oddly visceral loathing for homosexuals. I remember that he got a kick out of a newspaper story on some Marines beating up gays outside the base.

Liberal commentator TOM BRADEN, Patrick Buchanan's adversary on CNN's talk show "Crossfire"

I understand having to get out and fight for your rights — but please don't bring it into the drawing room, and please have a sense of humor about yourself.

JOAN RIVERS

———

Of course I didn't have to talk about my sexual preference in public. Of course taking on any label is self-limiting and wrong. But that's not the point. Because of my homosexuality I can't get a job as a coach. Unless certain attitudes change there's no way for me to function in this society doing what I want to do. If some of us don't take on the oppressive labels and publicly prove them wrong, we'll stay trapped by the stereotypes for the rest of our lives.

Former professional football player DAVE KOPAY, who came out publicly in a 1975 Washington Star *article on gay athletes*

———

Sometimes, you've got to close the door and tell the guys they suck. But I never tell them that they suck until I tell myself that *I* suck. You see, the way I look at it, we suck together.

Milwaukee Brewers' manager TOM TREBELHORN, on team meetings

———

In my plays I guess I have included every kind of sexuality but bestiality. But that's because I like animals too much.

TENNESSEE WILLIAMS

———

Now, if groups like Moral Majority have their way, there won't be any sex education at school, and our kids will be the dumbest in the world when it comes to sex . . . But our parents are sexually retarded too . . . Fear and primitive morals are creating a sexual pressure-cooker in this country and soon the top will blow . . . Only in the U.S. do we find children drawing a picture of a baby coming from the clouds or from under a cabbage leaf.

DR. FLOYD MARTINSON, professor of human sexuality at Gustavus Adolphus College in Minnesota

Producer Allan Carr: Spending his money carefully.

Murder is a crime. Describing murder is not. Sex is not a crime. Describing sex is.

Writer GERSHON LEGMAN

———

We are taught not to think decently on sex subjects, and consequently we have no language for them except indecent language.

GEORGE BERNARD SHAW

———

You don't spend $13 million to make a minority movie!

Producer ALLAN CARR, asked whether
Can't Stop the Music, *his 1980 film about the Village People, would have any gay overtones*

———

I love Annette Funicello movies ... as a matter of fact, if I could use any star in the world today, I would want Annette Funicello to star in my films ... I want her to play a crazed killer nymphomaniac.

JOHN WATERS

United Artists asked me what the story was, and I told them it was about this homosexual who married a nymphomaniac, and they said, "Great, go ahead!"

> *KEN RUSSELL, on his 1971 film biography of Tchaikovsky,* The Music Lovers

———

We want Rudi, especially in the nudi.

> *Chant taken up by dancer Rudolf Nureyev's fans at his performances*

———

The homosexual recognizes the homosexual as infallibly as the Jew recognizes the Jew. He detects him behind whatever the mask, and I guarantee my ability to detect him between the lines of the most innocent books.

> *JEAN COCTEAU (1889-1963)*

———

My lover has come back to me!

> *Mother of Japanese writer Yukio Mishima (1925-1970), upon hearing the news that her son had committed suicide*

———

Mothers precede all!

> *WALT WHITMAN*

———

Surely she will give up being dead now.

> *E.M. FORSTER, in despair shortly after the death of his mother*

———

My dead mother gets between me and life.

> *Artist ROMAINE BROOKS (1874-1970), when she was eighty-five*

———

For both good and bad, homosexual behavior retains some of the alarm and excitement of childish sexuality.

> *PAUL GOODMAN*

The diagnosis of homosexuality as a "disorder" is a contributing factor to the pathology of those homosexuals who do become mentally ill ... Nothing is more likely to make you sick than being constantly told that you are sick.

RONALD GOLD, former publicity director for the National Gay Task Force

———

In this town, a faggot is a homosexual gentleman who's had a few flops.

Anonymous gay television producer, quoted in TV Guide

———

I'm so tired of us not being allowed to touch each other, kiss each other, as straight people are allowed to do, as black people are allowed to do, as anybody else is allowed to do on TV. Every other minority has been exposed and dramatized to the hilt. Why are we kept in such straitjackets?

LARRY KRAMER, in a discussion of NBC's 1985 drama about AIDS, An Early Frost

———

As a recurrent theme, the movie stresses the love that blossomed between Michelangelo and Lorenzo the Magnificent's teenage daughter ... Though it may seem strange to the conventional minds of moviedom, this amorous relationship is more offensive to the knowledgeable spectator than the truth about Michelangelo's homosexuality.

From a 1965 article in Life *magazine about the film* The Agony and the Ecstacy

———

Give me a boy whose face and hand
Are rough with dust and circus-sand,
Whose ruddy flesh exhales the scent
Of health without embellishment;
Sweet to my sense is such a youth,
Whose charms have all the charm of truth;
Leave paints and perfumes, rouge, and curls,
To lazy, lewd Corinthian girls.

STRATO

If you're dealing with a gentleman for the first time, don't show off your full artistry by licking and tickling behind his balls, the length of his prick, etc. By acting less knowing, you'll give him a better impression of your past.

French poet and novelist PIERRE LOUŸS
(1870-1925)

———

For it falls to my lot, now and then, like the Caliph who used to roam the streets of Bagdad in the guise of a common merchant, to condescend to follow some curious little person whose profile may have taken my fancy. *Baron de Charlus, in MARCEL PROUST's* Cities of the Plain, *1922*

———

I'm drawn to older types, but that can't go on forever. When I'm ninety-eight I can't only be attracted to people in their hundreds.

NED ROREM

———

I delight in men over seventy. They always offer one the devotion of a lifetime. *OSCAR WILDE*

———

I'm now forty-three years old which, in faggot years, translates to a hundred and two. *Gay comic TOM AMMIANO*

———

It's the kind of picture you send to an old lover and say, "It's a good thing you left or look what you would have ended up with."

TRUMAN CAPOTE, on a picture taken of him in his fifties

———

When you get to be my age, that's when you really appreciate orgies, in the dark when nobody sees anybody and doesn't give a shit who they're being screwed by ... fat people, thin people, handsome people and ugly people, hunchbacks and one-legged people ... all together in the dark.

ALLEN GINSBERG

Gerry Studds: Another
reason to be proud.

The middle age of buggers is not to be contemplated without
horror.
                    VIRGINIA WOOLF (1882-1941)

Old friends are the great blessing of one's latter years.
                    HORACE WALPOLE (1717-1797)

Gay brothers and Gay sisters — that makes my toes curl. They
are not my brothers; and they are not my sisters! Some of them
are despicable, and I don't like them. And some heterosexuals are
despicable, and I don't like them. It is a false sense of community
... You come together to get that strength that comes only in
numbers, but you don't pretend that there is any superficial har-
mony that binds us together, other than the cause at hand.
                    JOHN RECHY

A glaring example of that is the Gay Activists Alliance, which sent

Andrew Holleran and Larry Kramer letters condemning their novels and the letter went out from the *media committee*. I don't know of any writer who could take seriously any criticism that comes from a group which includes literature under the title *media*.

> *Writer FELICE PICANO, on gay literature that is condemned, regardless of its artistic merits, on the grounds it is "politically incorrect"*

I've been targeted for defeat by everyone one would be proud to be targeted by.

> *Openly gay Congressman GERRY STUDDS (D-Massachusetts)*

Morality is simply the attitude we adopt toward people whom we personally dislike.

> *OSCAR WILDE*

Why do you think homosexuals are called fruits? It's because they eat the forbidden fruit of the tree of life . . . which is male sperm . . . There is even a Jockey short called Forbidden Fruit. Very subtle. Did you know that?

> *ANITA BRYANT*

Anita Bryant like Anita hole in the head.

> *Popular graffiti during the peak of Anita Bryant's anti-homosexual rights crusade*

I've never outraged Nature. I've always listened to her advice and followed it wherever it went.

> *JOE ORTON*

The laws of conscience, which we pretend to be derived from nature, proceed from custom.

> *French essayist MICHEL DE MONTAIGNE (1533-1592)*

Inside I had the feeling that I was a little girl. I preferred long hair and girl's clothes and didn't understand my parents treating me like a boy. I kept my feelings to myself. It's a good way to become cuckoo.

Transsexual WENDY CARLOS, who, as Walter Carlos, created the bestselling album Switched-On Bach *and the soundtrack score for* A Clockwork Orange. *In 1972, Carlos underwent the operation to become a woman; she went into seclusion and kept the operation a secret from the world until a 1979 interview in* Playboy. *She is now composing, recording, and giving concerts again.*

———

Some friends and I were out one night for a birthday celebration. We had some dinner and then decided to go to the old Park-Miller Theatre to see a porno movie. One guy fell asleep. I was laughing. They were playing "June Is Busting Out All Over" during a fuck scene; it was really hysterical. I said to my lover at the time, "Peter, why can't someone do a gay porn film that's serious?"

Gay porn filmmaker WAKEFIELD POOLE, on why he went into the porno business

———

I wouldn't suck your dick if I were suffocating and there were oxygen in your balls.

Line from the John Waters' cult classic Pink Flamingos

———

Through the nightly loving of boys, a man, on arising, begins to see the true nature of beauty.

PLATO

———

Most people who object to pederasty imagine the boy as a helpless stand-in for a girl. The image they have is of a brutal and powerful older man fornicating a boy who is biting his pillow and weeping into it as this terrible deed is being done to him, whereas, as we know, the real image is of a six-foot teenager who is being done by an older man who worships this young god and is probably paying him for it.

EDMUND WHITE

———

I'm disappointed there are no protestors here. Usually when I come to town, the kooks show up — the communists and Nazis and gays.

JERRY FALWELL,
at a 1985 press conference

———

Avoid, as you would the plague, a clergyman who is also a man of business.

ST. JEROME (c. 347-419)

———

I can't remember when I first began to notice that although all of the Mary Renault novels dealing with homosexual love in the Greece of Alexander the Great, of Plato, of Socrates and Theseus were joyous, even noble, the various modern novels I read about contemporary life among homosexuals always ended in pain and grief, a suicide in one, a betrayal in another, a murder, always a tragedy as an inevitable part of the story.

LAURA Z. HOBSON

———

It's not always like it happens in plays, not all faggots bump themselves off at the end of the story.

Michael, in MART CROWLEY's play
The Boys in the Band, *1968*

INDEX

Other books of interest from
ALYSON PUBLICATIONS

Don't miss our FREE BOOK offer at the end of this section.

☐ **THE GAY BOOK OF LISTS,** by Leigh Rutledge, $7.00. Leigh Rutledge has compiled a fascinating, informative and highly entertaining collection of lists that range from the historical (6 gay or bisexual popes) to the political (17 outspoken anti-gay politicians) and the outrageous (16 famous men, all reputedly very well-hung).

☐ **THE LITTLE DEATH,** by Michael Nava, $7.00. As a public defender, Henry Rios finds himself losing the idealism he had as a young lawyer. Then a man he has befriended — and loved — dies under mysterious circumstances. As he investigates the murder, Rios finds that the solution is as subtle as the law itself can be.

☐ **GOLDENBOY**, by Michael Nava, $15.00 (cloth). Gay lawyer-sleuth Henry Rios returns, in this sequel to Nava's highly-praised *The Little Death.*

Did Jim Pears kill the co-worker who threatened to expose his homosexuality? The evidence says so, but too many people *want* Pears to be guilty. Distracted by grisly murders and the glitz of Hollywood, can Rios prove his client's innocence?

☐ **WE CAN ALWAYS CALL THEM BULGARIANS: The Emergence of Lesbians and Gay Men on the American Stage,** by Kaier Curtin, $10.00. Despite police raids and censorship laws, many plays with gay or lesbian roles met with success on Broadway during the first half of this century. Here, Kaier Curtin documents the reactions of theatergoers, critics, clergymen, politicians and law officers to the appearance of these characters. Illustrated with photos from actual performances.

☐ **OUT OF ALL TIME,** by Terry Boughner, $7.00. Terry Boughner scans the centuries from ancient Egypt to modern America to find scores of the past's most interesting gay and lesbian personalities. He brings you the part of history they left out in textbooks. Imaginatively illustrated by Washington *Blade* artist Michael Willhoite.

☐ **BOYS' TOWN,** by Art Bosch, $8.00. Scout DeYoung's four basic food groups are frozen, bottled, canned, and boxed — but this warm-hearted story of two roommates who build an extended gay family is a gourmet's delight.

☐ **EXTRA CREDIT,** by Jeff Black, $6.00. Harper King's life consists of a boring job, stagnant relationships, and a tank full of fish named after ex-lovers, dying in the same order their namesakes were seduced. Now he decides he wants a fresh start in life — but life doesn't always cooperate.

☐ **AS WE ARE,** by Don Clark, Ph.D., 8.00. This book, from the author of *Loving Someone Gay*, examines gay identity in the AIDS era. Clark creates a clear and inspiring picture of where we have been, where we are going, and emphasizes the vital importance of being *As We Are*.

☐ **$TUD,** by Phil Andros; introduction by John Preston, $7.00. Phil Andros is a hot and horny hustler with a conscience, pursuing every form of sex — including affection — without apology, yet with a sense of humor and a golden rule philosophy. When Sam Steward wrote these stories back in the sixties, they elevated gay fiction to new heights; today they remain as erotic and delightful as ever.

☐ **MURDER IS MURDER IS MURDER,** by Samuel M. Steward, $7.00. Gertrude Stein and Alice B. Toklas go sleuthing through the French countryside, attempting to solve the mysterious disappearance of their neighbor, the father of their handsome gardener. A new and very different treat from the author of the Phil Andros stories.

☐ **REFLECTIONS OF A ROCK LOBSTER: A story about growing up gay,** by Aaron Fricke, $6.00. When Aaron Fricke took a male date to the senior prom, no one was surprised: he'd gone to court to be able to do so, and the case had made national news. Here Aaron tells his story, and shows what gay pride can mean in a small New England town.

☐ **A HISTORY OF SHADOWS,** by Robert C. Reinhart, $7.00. A fascinating look at gay life during the Depression, the war years, the Mc-Carthy witchhunts, and the sixties — through the eyes of four men who were friends during those forty years.

THE ALEX KANE BOOKS:

☐ No. 1: **SWEET DREAMS,** by John Preston, $5.00. In this, the first book of the series, Alex Kane travels to Boston when he hears of a ruthless gang preying on gay teenagers; in so doing he meets his future partner, Danny Fortelli.

☐ No. 2: **GOLDEN YEARS,** by John Preston, $5.00. Operators of a shady nursing home think they can make a profit by exploiting the dreams of older gay men — but they haven't reckoned with the Alex Kane factor.

☐ No. 3: **DEADLY LIES,** by John Preston, $5.00. Kane goes after a politician who's using homophobia to advance his own political career.

☐ No. 4: **STOLEN MOMENTS,** by John Preston, $5.00. Kane takes on a tabloid publisher in Texas, who has decided that he can take advantage of homophobia to increase his paper's circulation.

☐ No. 5: **SECRET DANGERS,** by John Preston, $5.00. Kane and his partner battle a world-wide terrorist ring that has made a specific target of gay tour groups.

☐ No. 6: **LETHAL SILENCE,** by John Preston, $5.00. Alex and Danny take on a wealthy businessman whose hatred of gay men threatens thousands of peaceful gay rights demonstrators.

☐ **THE MEN WITH THE PINK TRIANGLE,** by Heinz Heger, $6.00. In a chapter of gay history that is only recently coming to light, thousands of homosexuals were thrown into the Nazi concentration camps along with Jews and others who failed to fit the Aryan ideal. There they were forced to wear a pink triangle so that they could be singled out for special abuse. Most perished. Heger is the only one ever to have told his full story.

☐ **SAFESTUD: The safesex chronicles of Max Exander,** by Max Exander, $7.00. "Does this mean I'm not going to have fun anymore?" is Max Exander's first reaction to the AIDS epidemic. But then he discovers that safesex is really just a license for new kinds of creativity. Soon he finds himself wondering things like, "What kind of homework gets assigned at a SafeSex SlaveSchool?"

☐ **THE HUSTLER,** by John Henry Mackay; trans. by Hubert Kennedy, $8.00. Gunther is fifteen when he arrives alone in the Berlin of the 1920s. There he is soon spotted by Hermann Graff, a sensitive and naive young man who becomes hopelessly enamored with Gunther. But love does not fit neatly into Gunther's new life . . . *The Hustler* was first published in 1926. For today's reader, it combines a poignant love story with a colorful portrayal of the gay subculture that thrived in Berlin a half-century ago.

☐ **QUATREFOIL,** by James Barr, introduction by Samuel M. Steward, $8.00. Originally published in 1950, this book marks a milestone in gay writing: it introduced two of the first non-stereotyped gay characters to appear in American fiction. For today's reader, it remains an engrossing love story, while giving a vivid picture of gay life a generation ago.

☐ **BETTER ANGEL,** by Richard Meeker, $6.00. For readers fifty years ago, *Better Angel* was one of the few positive images available of gay life. Today, it remains a touching, well-written story of a young man's gay awakening in the years between the World Wars.

☐ **THE WINGS OF THE PHOENIX,** by Florine De Veer, $7.00. In this sequel to *Second Chances*, Mark Madison falls in love with a handsome young man named Blaise who has too many secrets. Little did he know what powerful forces would oppose their relationship.

☐ **LOVESEX: The horny relationship chronicles of Max Exander,** by Max Exander. Taking up where *SafeStud* left off, *LoveSex* tells of Exander's personal odyssey that results in establishing a lasting gay relationship which incorporates safer sex.

☐ **TALK BACK! A gay person's guide to media action,** $4.00. When were you last outraged by prejudiced media coverage of gay people? Chances are it hasn't been long. This short, highly readable book tells how you, in surprisingly little time, can do something about it.

☐ **THE TWO OF US,** by Larry Uhrig, $7.00. The author draws on his years of counseling with gay people to give some down-to-earth advice about what makes a relationship work. He gives special emphasis to the religious aspects of gay unions.

Get this book free!

Can Johnnie Ray Rousseau, a
22-year-old black singer, find
happiness with Keith Keller, a
six-foot-two blond bisexual jock
who works in a bank? Will Johnnie Ray's manager ever get him
on the Merv Griffin show? Who
was the lead singer of the
Shangri-las? *Eight Days a Week*,
by Larry Duplechan, answers
these and other silly questions,
while telling a love story as
funny, and sexy, and mem-
orable, as any you'll ever read.

If you order at least three other books from us, you may request a FREE
copy of this entertaining book. (See order form on next page.)

☐ **IN THE LIFE: A Black Gay Anthology,** edited by Joseph Beam,
$8.00. When Joseph Beam became frustrated that so little gay male
literature spoke to him as a black man, he decided to do something about
it. The result is this anthology, in which 29 contributors, through
stories, essays, verse and artwork, have made heard the voice of a too-
often silent minority.

☐ **LONG TIME PASSING: Lives of Older Lesbians,** edited by
Marcy Adelman, $8.00. Here, in their own words, women talk about
age-related concerns: the fear of losing a lover; the experiences of being a
lesbian in the 1940s and 1950s; and issues of loneliness and community.

☐ **UNBROKEN TIES: Lesbian Ex-Lovers,** by Carol Becker, Ph.D.,
$8.00. Lesbian relationships with ex-lovers are complex and unusual
ways of building alternative families and social networks. Carol Becker's
interviews with numerous pairs of ex-lovers tell the trauma of breaking-
up, the stages of recovery, and the differing ways of maintaining close
emotional connections with former lovers.

☐ **TO ALL THE GIRLS I'VE LOVED BEFORE, An AIDS Diary,** by J.W. Money, $7.00. What thoughts run through a person's mind when he is brought face to face with his own mortality? J.W. Money, a person with AIDS, gives us that view of living with this warm, often humorous, collection of essays.

To get these books:

Ask at your favorite bookstore for the books listed here. You may also order by mail. Just fill out the coupon below, or use your own paper if you prefer not to cut up this book.

GET A FREE BOOK! When you order any three books listed here at the regular price, you may request a *free* copy of *Eight Days a Week*.

- - - - - - - - - - - - - - . - -

Enclosed is $_____ for the following books. (Add $1.00 postage when ordering just one book; if you order two or more, we'll pay the postage.)

1. _____

2. _____

3. _____

4. _____

5. _____

☐ Send a free copy of *Eight Days a Week* as offered above. I have ordered at least three other books.

name: _____

address: _____

city: _____ state: _____ zip: _____

ALYSON PUBLICATIONS
Dept. H-40, 40 Plympton St., Boston, Mass. 02118

This offer expires Dec. 31, 1990. After that date, please write for current catalog.